"YOU ARE THE DAMNEDEST, MOST AGGRESSIVE FEMALE I'VE EVER MET!" GRIFF EXCLAIMED.

"I wanted to see what it would feel like to kiss you. I've thought about it a long time. . . ." Kyla felt her throat closing up and wondered if it was possible to choke to death over a simple kiss.

"And . . . ?" Griff prodded.

"Nice touch . . ." Kyla replied after a moment's consideration.

"I've never known a woman like you," Griff declared, shaking his head.

"You've never had a woman kiss you?"

"I've never had a woman make the first move before!"

"That's too bad. You've been missing out."

Suddenly Griff's powerful hands grasped her forearms, whipping her around to face him. "You want to know what it's like to kiss me, Kyla? That wasn't anything!"

CANDLELIGHT ECSTASY ROMANCES®

250 SUMMER WINE, *Alexis Hill Jordan*
251 NO LOVE LOST, *Eleanor Woods*
252 A MATTER OF JUDGMENT, *Emily Elliott*
253 GOLDEN VOWS, *Karen Whittenburg*
254 AN EXPERT'S ADVICE, *Joanne Bremer*
255 A RISK WORTH TAKING, *Jan Stuart*
256 GAME PLAN, *Sara Jennings*
257 WITH EACH PASSING HOUR, *Emma Bennett*
258 PROMISE OF SPRING, *Jean Hager*
259 TENDER AWAKENING, *Alison Tyler*
260 DESPERATE YEARNING, *Dallas Hamlin*
261 GIVE AND TAKE, *Sheila Paulos*
262 AN UNFORGETTABLE CARESS, *Donna Kimel Vitek*
263 TOMORROW WILL COME, *Megan Lane*
264 RUN TO RAPTURE, *Margot Prince*
265 LOVE'S SECRET GARDEN, *Nona Gamel*
266 WINNER TAKES ALL, *Cathie Linz*
267 A WINNING COMBINATION, *Lori Copeland*
268 A COMPROMISING PASSION, *Nell Kincaid*
269 TAKE MY HAND, *Anna Hudson*
270 HIGH STAKES, *Eleanor Woods*
271 SERENA'S MAGIC, *Heather Graham*
272 A DARING ALLIANCE, *Alison Tyler*
273 SCATTERED ROSES, *Jo Calloway*
274 WITH ALL MY HEART, *Emma Bennett*
275 JUST CALL MY NAME, *Dorothy Ann Bernard*
276 THE PERFECT AFFAIR, *Lynn Patrick*
277 ONE IN A MILLION, *Joan Grove*
278 HAPPILY EVER AFTER, *Barbara Andrews*
279 SINNER AND SAINT, *Prudence Martin*
280 RIVER RAPTURE, *Patricia Markham*
281 MATCH MADE IN HEAVEN, *Malissa Carroll*
282 TO REMEMBER LOVE, *Jo Calloway*
283 EVER A SONG, *Karen Whittenburg*
284 CASANOVA'S MASTER, *Anne Silverlock*
285 PASSIONATE ULTIMATUM, *Emma Bennett*
286 A PRIZE CATCH, *Anna Hudson*
287 LOVE NOT THE ENEMY, *Sara Jennings*
288 SUMMER FLING, *Natalie Stone*
289 AMBER PERSUASION, *Linda Vail*

LOVE'S DAWNING

Tate McKenna

A CANDLELIGHT ECSTASY ROMANCE®

Published by
Dell Publishing Co., Inc.
1 Dag Hammarskjold Plaza
New York, New York 10017

Copyright © 1984 by Mary Tate Engels

All rights reserved. No part of this book may be
reproduced or transmitted in any form or by any
means, electronic or mechanical, including photocopying,
recording or by any information storage
and retrieval system, without the written permission
of the Publisher, except where permitted by law.

Dell ® TM 681510, Dell Publishing Co., Inc.

Candlelight Ecstasy Romance®, 1,203,540, is a registered
trademark of Dell Publishing Co., Inc.,
New York, New York.

ISBN: 0-440-15020-5

Printed in the United States of America

First printing—December 1984

For my dear friends, Ed Nah and Madeline, the real designers and Desert Spirits, whose creativity inspired this story. And to Helen Hardin's beautiful art—may we always be Changing Women!

To Our Readers:

We have been delighted with your enthusiastic response to Candlelight Ecstasy Romances®, and we thank you for the interest you have shown in this exciting series.

In the upcoming months we will continue to present the distinctive, sensuous love stories you have come to expect only from Ecstasy. We look forward to bringing you many more books from your favorite authors and also the very finest work from new authors of contemporary romantic fiction.

As always, we are striving to present the unique, absorbing love stories that you enjoy most—books that are more than ordinary romance.

Your suggestions and comments are always welcome. Please write to us at the address below.

Sincerely,

The Editors
Candlelight Romances
1 Dag Hammarskjold Plaza
New York, New York 10017

CHAPTER ONE

*"Let the heavens be covered with banked-up clouds.
. . . Let thunder be heard over the earth."*

Evergreen-bedecked Corn Dancers filled the plaza between primitive pueblos and lifted up centuries-old pleas for rain and good summer crops. Chanting in unison, male singers murmured in an ancient Pueblo language. Beautifully adorned with brilliant feathers and cowrie shells, male dancers stamped and rattled gourds to waken the spirits and simulate rain. Earth mothers shuffled barefooted in the hot plaza dust, bedecked in black manta dresses and tablita headdresses, demonstrating the motions of grinding the much-desired corn. They wove impressive zigzag formations, lining up shoulder-to-shoulder, stepping to the loud cadence of a huge cottonwood drum. Solemn clowns, their breech-clothed bodies completely covered with paint and ash, appealed to Shiwana, the rain-cloud people. Their motions beckoned to the clouds, showing rain falling over *all the fields and how it would bring up a bountiful crop of corn.*

Griff watched the proud, statuesque old Indian as he walked as stealthily through the crowd as a young brave stalking an elusive buck. His ancient black eyes peered from a weathered face, regarding the fun-seekers and serious observers alike, skimming over the dark-skinned ones, scrutinizing the lighter ones. His job was to protect and preserve the integrity and beauty of the ceremony, a task he did not take lightly. On his chest he proudly bore the shiny tin star proclaiming Indian Police. He paused, hands on his hips, to observe the Corn Dance ritual. Briefly, his thoughts traveled back to another time, many moons ago. To the ancients . . .

Griff Chansler lifted his Stetson and wiped the perspiration from his brow with a muscled forearm, then replaced the hat. His brown eyes moved from the old Indian back to the dancers. They circled and hopped, keeping a primeval rhythm with the drums and shakers. For some of the dancers, the rhythm came more easily than others. But most of them followed exact trancelike motions with unmistakable precision.

Even though it was early in the day, the sun was unmerciful and beat down on the gathering as if to test the strength and dedication of the people watching. Griff felt a trickle of sweat between his broad-spread shoulder blades and hunched them so his shirt would absorb the moisture. There were times when such a big body was an encumbrance. Right now, it merely meant more area to sweat in this miserable heat. Another tiny stream rolled around his corded neck to his chest, mingling with the mat of dark hair. He shifted his six-foot, four-inch frame uncomfortably, thinking how refreshing a cool dip in the pool would be about now.

Abruptly a small flash of silver in the crowd diverted his attention from the dancers and shimmering heat of an unkind climate. Good God—who would have the nerve, the audacity to reveal a camera! But there it was! A clumsy thing in the hands of some idiot tourist with a flowered shirt and huge straw hat.

She took two snaps before the shadow of the old Indian stalker with the tin star badge moved over her. Griff smiled inwardly. She was doomed, and too ignorant to know it.

The Indian's walnut-brown hand closed over her lightly tanned wrist, and with his other hand he easily ripped the camera from her grasp. He stood before her, his proud countenance immobile, his lips thin with anger. Griff was close enough to hear his slightly-accented, terse words. "You must follow the rules and regulations if you stay here! No cameras allowed! There will be no photographs of the dancers!"

With a swift, easy motion, he opened the camera box and stretched the film out to its entire black length, exposing all of it.

A soft gasp of frustration escaped the woman's lips as the brown hands thrust the camera back toward her. "I'm sorry," she apologized. "It won't happen again." Her voice was precise, almost melodically soft —or was it hoarse from the embarrassment of being singled out from the crowd?

Griff couldn't help but notice that she was attractively slender. She stood as tall as the Indian man, which was probably around five feet, eight inches.

The proud Indian looked steadily at her for another long moment. His clothes were clean, but worn; a hot breeze whipped the loose ends of a red headband across straight, black hair. His penetrating eyes never wavered. It was obvious that he was defending far deeper values than any Anglo, especially such an insensitive tourist as this woman, could understand. The integrity of the ancients . . .

In the next moment, he pushed the camera into her hands. "Follow the rules and regulations or leave."

In her nervousness, the young woman dropped the small camera. It resounded on the hard desert earth with a dull thud, and she bent immediately to retrieve it. "I'm sorry if I've offended you," she replied weakly. "I'll put this away." She turned into the crowd and disappeared.

The dance continued, resounding drums and interspersing rattles not missing a beat. The brief scene between tourist and native had not disrupted anyone except the few people immediately around them. The old Indian moved to an obscure spot in the crowd to continue his vigilance. Griff lost sight of the attractive woman with the camera.

He tried to pay attention to the dancers again, but his eyes roamed through the crowd of their own accord. For some strange reason, probably just male curiosity, he tried to find the woman. The old Indian had shown leniency; perhaps she deserved worse. Sometimes the tribal members confiscated cameras and asked the perpetrators to leave.

This time, Griff's height was a definite asset as his brown eyes easily scanned over the top of the crowd. Then he spotted her leaning against an old adobe barn, fumbling with the camera. Why didn't she just put the damn thing away? Her head was bent and the huge straw hat completely shaded the upper part of her body. Beneath the sundress she wore, her legs were long and tanned and nicely shaped. Slim, bare feet wore skimpy leather sandals. For some crazy reason, the sight of her filled him with compassion. He couldn't understand why, and didn't stop to think about it. She looked so vulnerable. Inexplicably, he moved toward her.

When Griff's elongated shadow canopied her, she saw his boots first. Then her curious, sun-shaded eyes traveled upward, slowly. Scuffed, dusty cowboy boots. Long, blue-jeaned legs. Tight-fitted, hard thighs. A large, turquoise-studded belt buckle against a flat waist.

His hand, freckled with sun-bleached hairs scattered along the top, reached for the camera. "Let me see if it's broken. Surely you aren't stupid enough to reload it!"

She looked up at him quickly. Her oval face was practically covered with the huge, multifaceted sunglasses. The rest was protected from the sun by that awful straw hat; even her hair was covered with a purple scarf. "I beg your pardon?"

"I said, I don't think your camera's broken. Let me see it." Griff's hand was still extended and, with brief reluctance, she placed her camera there.

"Do you know anything about Minoltas? I hope it wasn't damaged when I dropped it." She was shaking slightly and a narrow ridge of perspiration beads lined the bridge of her nose. It was all Griff could do to keep from wiping those beads away.

He pursed his lips and examined the object that created her problem with the Indians. "I know a little about them. This one seems okay. Why did you bring it? You know it's forbidden. Against those ever-present rules and regulations. And why in hell would you try to take pictures in the middle of a dance?"

She shrugged and smiled with chagrin. "I thought a few snapshots wouldn't matter. Anyway, I wasn't trying to ruin the dance or defy their trust. Surely they still don't believe that nonsense about capturing their souls with a photograph. I just wanted to catch some of the Indian costumes. They're authentic and very beautiful."

Griff's walnut-brown eyes narrowed. "If everyone in the crowd had your cavalier attitude, this place would become a goddamn zoo! Tourists can be quite thoughtless. And sometimes the Indians respond somewhat rudely. You must realize that people have flocked to these ceremonials for years to gape curiously at something the Indians consider sacred. Religious. The rule is 'no cameras.' All you have to do is observe their rules, and everything will be fine. Don't you know anything about Indians?"

"Not much," she answered, tight-lipped. "Maybe someone like you, who is not so ignorant, could enlighten me."

Griff caught his breath. She was right! He wasn't an expert on Indians but at least he knew how to behave at their ceremonies. Who the hell was she, anyway? Already they were locking horns.

He spread one large palm. "Hell, what do I know? I'm no Indian. But, I do know that when you're on their land, you obey their rules. And, for Anglos, there's usually no slack. I've seen them confiscate cameras and ask offenders to leave the premises. You were lucky."

She smiled mockingly and white teeth flashed against her naturally tanned skin. "You make all this sound so ominous. There's no harm done. Just, no more pictures, that's all. They seem like friendly Indians to me. Not a scalper in the bunch."

He took a deep breath, determined not to let this woman pull him into her verbal traps. She was slick, all right. "Of course, it isn't dangerous here. I simply meant that you need to be careful whenever you're on Indian land. And observe the rules. The Indians are perfectly willing to share this sacred ceremony with you. The least you can do is to give them respect." He handed her the camera. "I suggest you put this away, out of sight. Incidentally, it was the white man who taught the Indians to scalp."

She accepted the camera with an indignant flip of her wrist and tucked it into her large canvas purse. "I'm sure you're right about all these Indian facts, but how do you suggest that I get pictures of some of these costumes? I need them for my business. It's very important to me."

He stuffed his fingers into tight jeans pockets, leaving thumbs out, and rocked back on his boot heels. "Well, now, I don't know. How badly do you need these photos?"

"If you'll get them for me, I'll pay you well."

Griff cocked his head. She was a determined female. And, judging from the way she talked and acted, definitely a tourist. "You must want them pretty badly."

"I do," she admitted honestly. "Somehow, I have

the feeling you know how to get them. For you, perhaps it would be a small feat. If it won't jeopardize your, ah, position in the community, I would make it worth your time and effort. You can use my camera. I have more film."

"Don't need it. I have my own." He looked skyward and wondered what in hell he was saying. Why had he admitted that? She was manipulating him, and he was allowing it!

"Well, then, do we have a deal? There are some special costumes here that I'd like on file. I'll show you which ones. The dancers don't have to be performing. I just want to see the intricacy of the designs on their costumes. They have given me some wonderful ideas already." Her voice lilted with enthusiasm.

Griff scrutinized the woman, but couldn't see past that awful, broad-brimmed hat with the brilliant purple scarf underneath, protecting her hair from the sun and hiding it from his view. Oh yes, she was obviously a tourist.

He couldn't even see her eyes, for they were covered with those huge, octagon-shaped sunglasses. And they were violet, for God's sake! He wondered if her eyes, too, were violet.

Up close, her flowered blouse wasn't flowers at all, but ferns and leaves on a backless sundress. *Backless and sexy!* It was cool green and white. Her shoulders were nice; her back, model-straight. The maleness in him appreciated that her correct posture thrust her breasts forward naturally. They seemed to be wrapped in smooth, green leaves. She looked very cool except for that row of perspiration beads on her nose. Griff was reminded of the sun beating unmercifully down on them and shifted his tall frame.

"A deal might be arranged." Why was he so goddamned willing? He didn't give a damn about her offer to pay. Or her, for that matter. So, why was he bothering? The questions lay unanswered in his mind.

"Might be? I thought you said you could do it!"

"Did I say that?"

"Yes, you indicated—"

"Take it easy, lady. Now is not the time to move. After that fiasco with the camera, you'd better stay put. You don't need any more scrutiny. The way you're dressed, you couldn't attract more attention if you wore a corn stalk on your head!"

She motioned angrily to the dancers with their evergreen-branch finery. "Looks to me like I'd blend right in!"

Griff rocked forward on his toes and leaned toward her. "Lady, you would never blend right in anywhere!"

She smiled, acknowledging that he had just given her a compliment, of sorts. "Thank you. Neither would you, Cowboy. Now, are you going to help me get the photos I need, or do I have to—"

"What we'll have to do," he interrupted rudely, "is take our time. And look for our chances." Griff turned his granite gaze toward the dancers, purposely trying to concentrate on their intricate movements. But he couldn't get his thoughts off the woman who stood impatiently beside him, shifting from one long leg to the other. *Long legs. Straight shoulders. Nice breasts. Sexy!* Damn! He had to get his mind on something else. Like the business at hand.

She sighed, loudly. "You Westerners are all alike! Wait and see. Wait and it'll happen. Wait and . . . everyone is on Mexican time around here. Wait until *mañana!*"

"Look, lady." Griff turned back to face her, shifting his thoughts from her attractive body parts to her verbal assault. "Do you want me to help you?"

"Of course. You said you would—"

"I said, shut up! And wait!" Damn! She was a pusher! Well, so was he!

The woman regarded him narrowly, through eyes practically hidden behind oversized, violet sunglasses, and folded her arms. What good would it do to argue with the surly bastard? If he was willing to help her, she would have to wait. With great effort, she stood beside him, silent and waiting.

Griff, too, folded his arms across a broad chest. He watched the next group of dancers, and waited. The heat seemed to intensify. Damn hot. He wondered why in hell he had walked over to this woman in the first place. And why he had agreed to help her. Perhaps it was only because it served his own purposes. But why did he have to drag her into it? There was just something about her . . .

Parts of the crowd started to move. Some people left, defeated by the heat. The dancers continued, and dark-skinned observers remained. They would never be defeated. Not by the heat, nor any aspect of nature. They were people of the earth.

Two streams of perspiration rolled around Griff's neck, converging into one aggravating rivulet in the middle of his back. Again he hunched his shoulders to absorb the moisture in the cool chambray shirt. He shifted and took a step. Surely they had waited long enough.

"How about some Indian fry bread? And a Coke?" He gestured toward the scraggly row of booths located along an ocotillo fence.

"The Coke sounds wonderful." She moved with him, stretching her stride to keep up with his long-legged pace.

He placed money on the counter and ordered, without further consulting her. "Two fry breads and two Cokes."

"Make mine a Tab," she amended, digging into her purse for change.

"Sure thing. But keep your money. This one's on me."

"Oh, no. Let me," she protested. "After all, you're taking—"

Griff's large palm stretched out to hush her. "No! Too late." He handed her the fry bread, liberally laced with honey, and the Tab. "It's already paid for."

"Thank you," she mumbled weakly. She had almost said too much. And she could tell this cowboy was none too pleased with her already. If she didn't watch her step, or mouth, he might not take the photos she needed. Then her whole day would be wasted, unless she wanted to try again. She gulped the Tab, then attempted lighter conversation. "Looks like the calories I saved with the Tab are heaped on this . . . this thing. Indian fry bread, you called it?"

"Yep." Griff ate silently, positive now that she wasn't from around this area. Everyone knew about fry bread. "A few calories won't hurt you."

"Is that supposed to be a compliment? I don't consider it as such." She ran a smoothing hand down her side in an unconscious gesture.

He ignored her female indignation. "You from around here?"

"No. I live in Tubac. In Arizona." She bit into the delicate, flat bread.

Griff's brown eyes glanced at her. "I'm from Tucson."

She licked a pearl of honey from the corner of her mouth. "You're right, though. I'm new. I've only been there three months."

Griff nodded, satisfied with his private assessment. He had known from the beginning she was a damned outsider. Glancing over the vacillating crowd, he searched, instinctively, for the old Indian who had caught his eye earlier. Another row of dancers stood outlined against the startlingly clear blue sky, awaiting their turn at the dance. This should be enough time.

"Come on," Griff muttered to the woman as he started through the edge of the crowd.

"Wait a minute." Her soft hand rested on his muscled forearm. "Do you mind an introduction? After all, we have a business deal going. And we've shared a Coke and Indian fry bread. I'm Kyla Tramontano."

In an instinctively polite gesture, he touched the brim of his Stetson. "Griff Chansler." *Tramontano?* His walnut eyes flickered over her again. With a name like that, she could easily be a local native. But she sure as hell didn't act like one. And she admitted to being new in the area. "Come with me, Ms. Tramontano. We're going around back."

She hesitated. "Griff? May I call you Griff?"

He shrugged. "Sure. Call me anything."

She smiled, attempting to break the hard shell around him. "Then call me Kyla. Could we cut this tough-guy, frontier attitude and work together on a friendlier, first-name basis?"

Griff's lips twitched annoyingly. "Anything you say, . . . Kyla." She was damned assertive! Why was he helping her if she made him so damned antagonistic? And why did he feel that way? She had done nothing to warrant his belligerent attitude. Nothing except assert her opinions. He was, in fact, the one who had approached her. The aggressor.

"Let's go, then." Kyla took two steps ahead, then stopped to wait for him. After all, she really didn't know where they were going. "You lead the way, Griff."

Griff swallowed a smile and proceeded ahead of her. They circled a couple of brown adobe buildings, rounded dusty, ocotillo corrals, and stopped near a small group of gaily-dressed dancers.

"Any of these?" Griff muttered closely.

"Yes. The girl in the white leather dress with the marvelous beadwork. And those with the beautiful headdresses."

"Stay here," he instructed testily. "I'm going to see if I can capture a few souls."

Kyla watched as Griff spoke quietly to the gathering of dancers, pointed to the chosen few, then dug into his pocket and handed each something. With practiced skill, he posed the performers and quickly snapped a dozen photos. He consulted with Kyla, succinctly following her directions. Other dancers came and went. Griff dealt with them quickly, patiently, professionally. If they declined, he accepted it without hassle.

Kneeling or stooping in the dust, Griff went about his task with serious dedication, oblivious to the irritating heat that steamed from the baked earth. His shirt clung damply to his muscled frame. By the time he was finished, the light blue material was almost completely dark with perspiration.

"There. That should do it, shouldn't it?" He ambled to the shaded corner where Kyla stood, waiting quietly.

"Yes." Kyla nodded with no small amount of admiration. "That's more than adequate. I can't tell you how much I appreciate this, Griff. Now, how much do I owe you? You set the price, and I'll write a check." She began to dig into the purse.

He shrugged and dropped the small camera back into his breast pocket. "Don't know yet. Why don't you stop by my shop next week and see which ones you want? We'll settle on it then."

"Oh. You mean you'll develop them, too? I'll be glad to do that, Griff. I hadn't planned on you going to all that trouble."

"No trouble. Here's my business card. Stop by about Thursday. They'll be ready by then." He handed her a small, ecru card, then tipped his hat and wheeled on his booted heel. As he walked away, a small dust devil whirled in one of his footsteps.

Griff opened the hot, metal door to one of a hundred pickup trucks in the parking area. Sliding onto the scorching plastic seat, he endured the fiery stinging that radiated through his jeans. It was expected torture in this Arizona heat. He drove away in a cloud of dust, puzzling why in hell he had allowed himself to get involved with that woman. Who was she, this woman with the strange outfit and violet eyes? *Kyla Tramontano.* The name rolled around in his mind. And why was she here at the Indian dances?

She was an attractive woman, with shapely legs and nice shoulders. *Sexy!* But he had approached her before he actually evaluated her physical attributes. Maybe it was the vulnerability about her that tugged at him. And yet, she was the damnedest female he'd been around in a while. She had a mind of her own, and a strong one at that. Maybe he'd better steer clear of her. Involvement with that woman—any woman— he could do without. Well, that would be easy enough. He'd let Pasqual or Mavis take care of her when she came for the photos next Thursday.

Griff forced the woman with the violet eyes out of his mind as he noted the dark, banked-up clouds which appeared over the mountain peaks. They billowed and expanded rapidly. Distant thunder rumbled threateningly and forked flashes of desert lightning promised a rare spring rain.

Shiwana, the rain-cloud people, must be smiling.

CHAPTER TWO

Kyla Tramontano parked beside the sprawling khaki-colored plaster office building, so unlike the familiar towering Chicago skyscrapers. She fumbled in her purse for the ecru card. Chansler Marketing, Inc. It matched the wording on the large building before her, the place he had called his "shop." *Griff Chansler.* His name sent a feminine thrill through her. It sounded strong and powerful. She smiled to herself . . . the strong, silent type. He wasn't exactly silent, but certainly not what you would call talkative. She recalled, with inner pleasure, the man's tall, rugged appearance. Western attire. Muscular and masculine. A very appealing cowboy. Yes, he would be an interesting man with whom to conduct her business.

Kyla stepped out into the crisp desert morning air and adjusted her skirt. The dress was her own design, a contemporary version of the Indian *manta,* off one shoulder. It fit her tall, slender frame perfectly, and

Kyla felt good in it. She tucked a dark strand of hair into the chignon at the back of her neck and entered the building.

The bold decor in the spacious entranceway made a definite Southwest statement in browns and blues. Prints by Peña and Gorman were interspersed with Papago baskets and miniature Navajo blankets. Another dynamic painting caught her eye and drew her close. The colors and lines and energy visible in the modern adaptation of a female figure captured Kyla for a moment, then her eyes dropped to the signature. *Tsa-sah-wee-eh.* Beneath the strange Indian name was the name of the work and artist. *Changing Woman* by Helen Hardin.

Kyla smiled to herself. *Changing woman . . .* that's me. Perhaps it's any woman who grows. Inevitable changes must take place with growth. The strength of the painting reached Kyla in an almost tangible way, and she let her eyes travel again over the flowing, colorful lines of *Changing Woman.*

Kyla turned to the receptionist, who had watched her reaction. "It's . . . it's beautiful."

"Yes, it is," the woman responded eagerly. "Helen Hardin was a well-known New Mexico artist. Her work always had a certain power. *Changing Woman* speaks to all women. In Navajo mythology, Changing Woman is an important deity. She was the creator and her spirit is still strong in many people's lives." The receptionist paused to answer the phone, then gave Kyla her attention again. "I'm sure you didn't come for an art lesson. May I help you?"

Kyla nodded. "I would like to speak with Griff

Chansler, please. But thanks for telling me about Changing Woman."

"My pleasure." The woman smiled amiably. "What time is your appointment?"

"I don't have a specific appointment, but he's expecting me sometime today," Kyla answered confidently. "Just tell him that Kyla Tramontano is here to see the photographs he took for me at the Indian dances."

"One moment please. Just have a seat." The young woman murmured an inaudible message into her headphone.

In a few minutes a trim-suited, tight-faced woman approached. "Ms. Tramontano? Mr. Chansler is busy at the moment and asked me to help you. I'm Mavis Dobson."

Kyla felt a distinct disappointment at not seeing Griff again. Damn! Why wouldn't he see her? "I . . . I was supposed to pick up some photographs he took for me the other day," she explained weakly.

"Oh, yes. I know about those. Please come this way." Mavis Dobson led the way past the receptionist's desk to an expansive room, filled with various noisy printing and copy machines. A long counter separated the work area from the customers. Mavis smiled indulgently at Kyla, a plain woman tolerating one who is very attractive. With a swift motion, she served the photos over the counter as if they were an order of two eggs and ham.

Deep inside, Kyla balked. Why was she doing this? Allowing Mavis—and Griff—to manipulate her like this! She sifted through the prints absently, having difficulty keeping her mind on the reasons she came here.

The photos. That's why she came, isn't it? *No!* she decided suddenly. *I came to see this intriguing cowboy, Griff Chansler, and, by God, I will! I have business with him!* Neatly, Kyla stacked the photos back together, her fingers working precisely with the slick black and whites. "I think I'll wait and evaluate these with Gr— Mr. Chansler."

Ms. Dobson stared, her no-nonsense expression stiff.

Kyla stared back and smiled indulgently. "I would like an appointment with Mr. Chansler today."

"I beg your pardon? Are you dissatisfied with the photos?" Mavis Dobson's eyes penetrated. "Incidentally, he said there'll be no charge."

"No. They're fine. I would just like to see him."

Mavis rushed to explain again, "Mr. Chansler is busy now. He said you could just take the photos—"

"Well, I can't. I need to speak to him about some business." Kyla smiled tightly, knowing that if she didn't stand firm, this Mavis Dobson would be assigned to her, and she might never see him again. That possibility was unsettling her.

"Very well. I'll see what I can do. He's with a client now. You might have to wait awhile." Mavis' lips grew tight, and she managed to sound very official.

Kyla nodded curtly and sounded very official herself. "I'll wait." Changing Woman would approve.

If Kyla hadn't been such a strong individual, she probably would have crumbled under Mavis Dobson's glare alone. She gathered her photos and determinedly followed Mavis back to the receptionist's desk.

Before she even had a chance to sit and wait, Kyla heard him. Although she had talked to the man only briefly that day at the Indian dances, the timbre of his voice was imprinted in her mind. *He* was imprinted on her mind. In fact, she had thought of little else except this impressive man, this cowboy, during the entire, long week. She turned toward the sound of his voice, and matched surprised expressions with the tall man she had waited so impatiently to see. He wasn't at all what she expected!

Dressed in a dark pinstripe suit, he was no cowboy today. The dark business apparel framed his huge squareness, and Griff Chansler loomed like a solid rock, stable and stalwart. He exuded authority today, and a maleness that was impossible to ignore. His face was the same square-jawed impression she remembered, his nose straight, his brown eyes alert, his hair —my God! A thick shock of dashing, dominant, dark auburn hair! Kyla had never seen hair quite like that, auburn with a hint of brown. Like russet tapestry, rich and bronze! He was a man of distinctive shapes and colors!

"Griff?" Kyla was almost too shocked to speak. Since he had worn his Stetson that day at the Indian dances, she hadn't seen his hair. Somehow, she imagined him with black or brown hair, but not red! Actually, it wasn't red. It was auburn. More a deep burgundy . . .

"Yes?" He handed a folder to Mavis and gazed with masculine appreciation at the tall, jet-haired woman dressed in the yellow *manta*. Her skin was a smooth, golden topaz, reminding him of a wild fawn, and very touchable. With that off-one-shoulder dress, there was certainly enough skin visible to admire its satiny beauty. She knew him; had called him by name. But, for the life of him, Griff couldn't recall where he had met this gorgeous woman. Surely he would have remembered her! He stalled for time. "Can I help you?"

Kyla smiled eagerly. "I hope so. Could I see you for a moment, Griff?"

Mavis interceded sharply, "Mr. Chansler, I told Ms. Tramontano that you have another appointment at ten-thirty."

If Kyla was surprised to grasp the full picture of Griff Chansler, he was astounded by her image. After all, he hadn't seen *any* of her on the day of the dances, except legs and shoulders and breasts! Was this the woman who had requested his photographic services and seemed so vulnerable? The woman he belittled and bossed and introduced to fry bread! This was the woman who hid behind a scarf and hat and violet sunglasses? Well, her eyes weren't violet at all, but a dark, delicious, chocolate brown. The fry bread hadn't hurt her figure one bit. And she seemed very capable today, not shy or vulnerable.

Griff extended a large hand and grabbed hers. "Of course, Kyla! You caught me off guard for a minute. I'll be glad to see you this morning. Right now, in fact." He didn't release her hand, but tugged her along the hall calling out instructions to "Hold my calls" to the receptionist.

Mavis glared, foiled in her attempts to keep Griff's office hours running smoothly, as the two disappeared into his paneled office. He usually kept his private life out of the office. But this pushy female was different! She didn't belong here.

The door closed, giving them the privacy they both sought. Griff politely seated Kyla and offered her coffee, deciding to sit in the near chair, instead of across the wide expanse of desk from her.

"It's good to see you, Kyla. See you again, that is. Did you look at the photographs? Are they satisfactory? I must admit, I'm not much of a photographer, and our conditions that day weren't optimum." He pressed his long body into the chair meant for people of average height, folding his legs until his knee rested disarmingly close to hers.

Curiously, Kyla watched Griff, wondering if he would strip out of that suit any minute, Superman style, and become the denim-jeaned cowboy she had first met. Somehow, this was not the man she had fantasized about all week. "Well, you certainly managed far better than I did that day. At least you kept your film. The photos are fine. I can't tell you how much I appreciate your help. And I plan to pay for it."

He shrugged and admitted truthfully, "You owe me nothing, Kyla. It was indeed my pleasure. How can I help you today?"

"I need your advice. Maybe your services."

"Oh?"

"Professional services, of course," she amended. "You see, I'm starting a new business, designing distinctive Southwest Indian clothes for the mass market. I need to know how to start, how to sell my ideas, and where."

He smiled. "You've come to the right place. Marketing is our specialty. We also do general printing of all kinds and some layouts. I'd be glad to help you—"

"No," she resisted, smoothing her skirt with a topaz-colored hand. "Let's get something straight right up front. I want to become a client of Chansler Marketing. I want our association to be legitimate business. No more freebies."

He pursed his lips and allowed his eyes to follow the curve of her hip down the length of her dress to those spectacular legs. "Of course. We can arrange that. Is this," he gestured to her apparel, "one of your creations?"

"Yes." She smiled proudly, squaring her shoulders, one daringly, sexily bare. "It's called a *manta,* originally from the Hopi Indians. It's a very cool, comfortable dress. I think if it's marketed the right way, women will buy it."

"Well, yours certainly has appeal," he assessed.

"The problem is getting it out to the public," she explained, noting the admiration in his eyes.

"That's where we come in. We set up media appearances, do all your PR, and work up a marketing plan designed specifically for you."

"Sounds terrific. How do we start?"

"Well, it depends on how you want to work—consignment, commission, or special orders, and how far along in your organization you are. We need to set up an appointment and arrange for photographs of your designs, preferably on models. Then we need to prepare a portfolio." He reached a long arm across the desk for a brochure and printed form.

Kyla was filled with hope and expectation. This man seemed to know what he was talking about. And he made sense. Oh yes, this was one of her better decisions. Chansler Marketing would do exactly what she needed to get her business off the ground. "Looks like

I'm going to be pretty busy in the near future. I have a lot of work to do before we start."

He handed her the papers. "Read this brochure. It explains how we work, plus the decisions you must be prepared to make. And a general time frame. Of course, we'll make a time frame with individual goals designed for your specific organization at the next visit. Stop by the reception desk and make an appointment. Then fill out the form before your first appointment, and we'll go from there."

Kyla stood and extended her hand. "Thank you, Griff. I think the best thing that happened to me was the day my film was exposed at the Indian dances. At the time, I was deeply humiliated. But now, I'm glad it happened because you saved the day. Now, you're going to launch my business. I'm extremely pleased."

Griff towered beside her, drinking in her feminine beauty, barely hearing what she said. He was taken by her poise, captured by the fine lines of her face, mesmerized by her enticing skin. Oh yes, it would be a pleasure doing business with Kyla. Perhaps making love to her. *Oh my God—what am I thinking?*

"Glad to know we can help. I'll see you again soon, Kyla." He looked into her dark brown eyes and felt himself miring in their depths.

She turned and left, smiling at the *Changing Woman* painting on the way. There was a sense of elation in her spirit . . . of changing and growing. Of enhanced self-esteem.

For some crazy, weird reason, Kyla's appearance and entreaty for his professional assistance had plunged Griff into the dourest of moods. He paced the confines of his richly paneled office, angry at himself for letting this woman intrigue him. And yet, the attraction was there. He couldn't help it. But could he steer the situation in the direction he wanted? What did he want? Nothing more than a casual affair, for sure!

Griff Chansler stuffed his hands in his pockets and glared out the window. In a moment a lovely Indian princess with delicate features, high cheekbones, and beguiling, silky fawn skin glided to her car. She bent to open the door, and the yellow *manta* hitched to reveal a nice portion of shapely, tanned leg.

Fawn-colored. He wondered, wildly, if her skin was that soft, golden tone all over. What would she be like in bed? Suddenly, his slacks tightened against his thighs as her feminine appeal attacked his masculine control. *My God—I'm at it again! I have to get her off my mind!*

One definitive way to do that was to get her out of his life. Griff couldn't let himself get involved, in any way, with someone like her. Wouldn't. He'd see to it that Pasqual took care of her first appointment.

Kyla turned her old car south on I-19 and fairly flew home. Her head swirled with the expectations of what Griff Chansler had said to her. Her business, so long a dream, seemed closer to becoming a reality than ever. Oh, how she wanted it to be a success! Not only because it was her love, but because these Indian designs were so special, so unique. They perpetuated an art that previously had been passed down from mother to daughter, but was being lost to modern generations. Now, with her designs for the mass market, the Southwest Indian designs could be preserved forever. The beauty wouldn't die with the young, who moved away from their culture and forgot such intricate beauty. They would be everlasting, like this *manta* she wore. Like Changing Woman, ever changing, ever growing, yet lasting forever.

Kyla thrilled to think she would be the one to perpetuate them. With help from Griff.

Griff Chansler. She mulled the man over in her mind. He was not what she expected. Not at all. He was more businesslike, less casual Western. She chided herself. Was she disappointed, just slightly, perhaps, that he had abandoned his Western attire? There was some mystique about the Western man. The strong, silent cowboy.

Admittedly, she had been intrigued with the brusque manner and rugged looks of the man at the Indian Reservation who had suddenly appeared at her side to help her salvage her bruised ego. Then he had enhanced the initial attraction she'd felt for him by disappearing in a whirl of dust. Yes, Kyla had to confess. She was attracted to a mystical Griff Chansler.

One short hour's drive south of Tucson was nestled the sleepy little artists' colony and historical settlement of Tubac that Kyla now called home. It had been a strange but immediate meshing between the Chicago-bred, professional designer and the lazy, Spanish-influenced community of Tubac. It had been love at first sight.

Within weeks of her first visit, Kyla had flown back to the windy city and begun making plans to quit her job and move. It took her a month; a miserable, snow-plagued month, to train a replacement, pack her personal belongings, and sell every Midwestern ounce of furniture. She wanted to come to Arizona burden-free, ready for the newness here. And she had never regretted a moment of her rash, hasty decision. Yes, she was indeed Changing Woman.

Kyla turned off the highway and down the road that took her back in time. The humble adobe that housed her fledgling business in the front room and her suitcases and bed in back beckoned her, like no classy, high-rise apartment ever could. This was a back-to-basics life, drawing on her earthy desires, inducing her by some unknown yearning. Perhaps it was her heritage, so carefully hidden until recently. . . .

"Hi, Madeline!" Kyla called to her friend before she was out of the car. "Guess what! He's going to take me on as a client, and tell me exactly what to do to get this business started, and he knows just what to do! It's going to be wonderful! This is what we've been looking for, what we've needed!" She hugged Madeline's withered shoulders, and showed her the brochure from Chansler Marketing.

"Does he know anything about the retail business?" Madeline's cautious mind accepted nothing at face value as she scanned the brochure.

"He knows everything . . . well, everything about his business, which is making other people's businesses work. Oh, it's so exciting! Come on in, and I'll tell you everything he said." Kyla led her older friend through the back door and started preparing glasses of iced tea while Madeline read over the brochure.

"I haven't seen you so excited about anything in a long time, Kyla," Madeline commented as she listened and watched Kyla's dark eyes dance.

"I don't know when I've been so excited. This is something substantial that I can do to get my business going. Griff, er . . . Chansler Marketing knows the business end like I never could. I'll take care of the designing, but he knows marketing. And, oh, it's so important!"

"I see." Madeline nodded slowly, observing the animation of her usually placid friend. "You've needed this, Kyla."

"You bet I have! Now, we can concentrate on the designing! I'm going to hire that seamstress I talked to last week, and the Indian woman you know. She can do some beadwork and appliqués. It's rolling now!" Kyla forced herself to sit at the table, barely able to control her high energy level.

Madeline smiled. "Good. That's good."

A concerned look crossed Kyla's face. "How are you feeling today, Madeline? You're not sick again, are you?"

"No, dear. I'm just a little tired. Didn't rest very well last night. Those damned coyotes kept me awake. One of the disadvantages of living in the country." She smiled weakly.

Kyla stoutly defended her new home. "One of the very few disadvantages, I might add. I didn't hear a thing. Slept like a log. And it was so cool, I had to grab a blanket! Maybe you could take a nap later, Madeline. I'll watch your shop for you."

Madeline shook her head with a smile. "Thank you, no. I'll be all right. I've never seen anyone take to Arizona the way you have, Kyla. You won't even admit anything's wrong with the place. Just wait until this summer and the temperature reaches a hundred and ten degrees! Your enthusiasm will wilt soon enough!"

Kyla grinned at the woman she admired and considered to be her mentor. "Why, Madeline, this is all your fault. If you hadn't been out here, I would never have come to Arizona. It could as easily have been Sun City or Miami or . . . or Boise. I would have visited you anywhere."

"Arizona was chosen for health reasons. I was just lucky to find Tubac instead of Sun City."

"I'm lucky you found it, too. You said people either hated the place and left, or loved it and stayed forever. I happened to fall in the latter category! I can guarantee though that I would never have fallen in love with Boise! Not enough sun for me," Kyla admitted fervently. "And, without your encouragement and the inspiration of the cultures here, I would never have gone into business for myself. This particular business, anyway."

"Oh yes, you would. You have too much creativity to have stayed at Market Design much longer," Madeline countered.

Kyla shrugged. "I spent five years there. That's a long time. I'll admit I learned a lot about design. But the best thing that came out of those five years was knowing you and all you taught me, Madeline."

"Nonsense! You're a smart gal. You would have picked it up without me."

"Without you, I probably would have quit the business. I almost did when Mom died. You were already out here, and life in the city just became unbearable." Kyla's tone grew dull. The last year of her life had been filled with grief and sadness and loneliness. It probably made the present all the brighter and gave her renewed incentive to enjoy each day to the fullest.

Madeline admitted seriously, "Every day I'm glad you moved here, Kyla. You have cheered my life in countless ways since your arrival."

Kyla patted Madeline's arthritic, gnarled hand. "Well, I've certainly thrown some complications into it!" They laughed together, and Kyla thought briefly how those misshapen hands had once designed some of the finest clothes in the world. Then arthritis crippled them, progressively and painfully. Madeline was forced to make a living where she could. That was when Kyla met her. Madeline was on her way down in the fashion world, and Kyla was a young designer with fresh ideas on her way up.

Their friendship grew from mutual respect. Kyla knew that locked inside those crippled hands was more skill and ability than could be found in twenty of the most beautiful. So Kyla learned from Madeline, continued to draw from her rich reservoirs of knowledge and experience, and tried to help her in whatever ways she could.

"You've given me something to look forward to each day, Kyla. My life would be dull without your constant commotion. Now, tell me about him. This Griff." She nodded with eager interest.

"Griff? Oh, he's just a man I met." Kyla shrugged and ran a finger around the edge of her tea glass.

"No, he isn't just any man," Madeline chided. "Not the way your eyes light up when you talk about him. What is he like? Is he tall?"

Kyla turned up an amused face and professed dramatically, "He has red hair! Actually, it's deep, dark auburn. Like russet tapestry."

"Red hair?" Madeline mused. "Sounds fascinating."

"Not red! Auburn! On him, it's very attractive. He's smart and tall and very Western. Probably a little too macho for me, though."

"They make 'um too macho for you, Kyla?" Madeline teased.

"Out here in the West, they do. You know what I mean, Madeline. This Griff Chansler is kingpin in his own little world. The only reason I like him is because he will make it possible for my business to take off. That's exciting!"

Madeline scrutinized her younger friend. "Are you sure that's your only reason for being intrigued, Kyla? This Griff Chansler sounds like someone more important to you than that."

"No, Madeline." Kyla shrugged. "I've only met the man twice. Anyway, I'm not looking for a man. And, if I was, he wouldn't be a red-haired, macho cowboy."

"What would he be like?" Madeline challenged.

Kyla thought for a moment. "The strong, silent type."

CHAPTER THREE

"I know why he's doing this to me! He thinks my business isn't legitimate! He thinks I'm a fly-by-night female dabbling in the business world, and he doesn't want to bother with me! To him, I'm a foreigner because I haven't lived here in Arizona forever! He doesn't know I'm a native of the desert! He's too busy to tend to me personally! At least, that's what they told me. Mavis Dobson took great pride in that! What an old witch! I don't know why he has someone like her working for him! She probably runs more customers off than can battle her sourpuss face!" Kyla paused briefly in her tirade to look at an indulgent Madeline.

"I'm sure she's very competent," Madeline observed quietly. "Or he wouldn't have her working there."

"Well, I don't like her. Thank God I didn't have to deal with Mavis! I would have just walked out and taken my business elsewhere! Mr. Griff Chansler, you would have lost a potentially prosperous, moneymaking customer!" Kyla issued her verbal barrage to an invisible entity, before lifting the heavy bolt of handdyed material to a display rack. She bent again to the box and lifted another, exerting more angry energy than was necessary for the chore. However, the energy was there, bottled up all morning after her first appointment with Chansler Marketing, Inc.

Madeline followed her, folding the end of the bolted material back, lovingly shaping it for best display of the color and design. The swollen knots at each knuckle were painful reminders of why she was here in this dry desert land. Quietly she prodded, "Who did you talk to?"

Kyla heaved another bolt and adjusted it. "Someone named Pasqual. He was nice enough. He just wasn't . . ."

"Griff Chansler," Madeline inserted placidly, voicing the real reason for Kyla's frustration.

"Frankly, yes. I . . . Griff's the first one I talked to about this marketing business, and the one with whom I feel most comfortable. I don't like being shuffled around." Kyla spewed out her reasons, testing them on Madeline, trying to see if they sounded rational. She had spent the last hour driving back from Tucson recounting the justification for her extreme agitation about the whole matter.

Madeline wisely refrained from judging the reasonableness of Kyla's fury. In fact, she added a motive of her own. "Well, after all, Griff is the head honcho at Chansler Marketing. He is the pro, and you want the most for your marketing money." Her crippled fingers caressed the material, straightening it to her satisfaction after Kyla had plunked each bolt unattractively on the counter rack.

Kyla pushed dark wisps of hair back and wiped her forehead. "Oh, Pasqual seemed to know what he was talking about. Said I needed to work on a photo portfolio with a professional photographer doing the layout. It isn't a job for me and my automatic Minolta. I guess he's right," she sighed.

"Do you have to hire a professional photographer?"

"No. Pasqual can take the pictures. Or Griff." Kyla was suddenly quiet, like a churning, puffing engine who had run out of steam. The last of the heavy bolts of material was placed, and she rested her hands on it, absently caressing the linen texture. She gazed out the square-paned window of the quaint historic building and concentrated on the vacilatting branches of a nearby cottonwood tree.

"Now, that would be nice. If Griff came out to photograph your work, I could meet the man," Madeline deducted sensibly.

"So could I," Kyla muttered. "Actually, Madeline, I know very little about him. I've barely met him. But he . . ." Her words drifted as she again watched the willowy tree limbs battling a sudden gust.

"You don't have to explain to me, Kyla. Let's face it. The man is attractive and he appeals to you." Madeline eyed her new material display. Then, satisfied, she moved behind the sales counter.

"No, he doesn't appeal to me! He's too macho. And not nearly suave enough for me. I prefer a man who's more worldly and has more respect for women. For the modern, changing woman. Griff doesn't seem to even be aware of the modern woman. I'm probably the first one he's ever encountered." Kyla stoutly resisted the idea that she was attracted to him, yet toyed with the notion that he did interest her.

Madeline's blue eyes cut sharply, as did her words. "A more worldly man? Like Ian?"

Kyla's face sobered. "No. Not like Ian. Not at all." Mentally, she mused that her attraction to Griff Chansler was due in part to the obvious fact that he was different from Ian de Baer in every way. It was her own inner rebellion to the man who had used her. Thoughts of Ian brought a sour taste to her mouth and sent a chill through her.

"Perhaps the only way Griff can deal with a woman like you, Kyla, is to pawn you off to someone else! Have you considered that?" Madeline posed with a laugh.

Kyla's thoughts switched from Ian, and she reconsidered Griff. "You're probably right! That's exactly what I think he's doing! Pawning me off with someone like Pasqual who isn't threatened." Kyla's voice rose with agitation at the thought.

"Well, why don't you show him what the modern woman is like? Even though you have a head on your shoulders, you aren't threatening to his masculinity."

"His mas—Oh, Madeline! No one threatens this man's masculinity! He's the epitome of virility!"

Madeline raised her eyebrows and began to leaf through a new wholesale catalog. "Oh? Obviously you've threatened something."

"That's ridiculous! I haven't done a thing! Not yet, anyway!" Kyla grinned devilishly.

A small smile creased Madeline's lips as she perceived the fighting feminine instinct rising in Kyla.

"Well then, if he's so secure, invite him down here, and let me meet him. Maybe he'd be interested in an older woman."

"Madeline!" Kyla laughed at her friend's boldness. "What about Wade?" she asked, referring to Wade Spencer, a wealthy widower who sought out Madeline's companionship. Like Kyla, he saw beyond her crippled hands and enjoyed her zest for life.

Madeline's blue eyes danced with devilment, and she shrugged her slender shoulders. "Wade's a wonderful man, but he's of the older set. Griff would keep me young! I think I could handle them both!"

Kyla propped her hands on her slim hips and smiled. "Madeline, you're amazing! I love your spirit, but doubt your capability! Two men, indeed! Are you threatening that if I don't pursue Griff Chansler, you will?"

Madeline glamorously raised her hand to fluff her short, curly, gray-streaked hair, then lapsed into a Mae West impression. "Hmmm. Something like that. Why don't you come on over to my place sometime, big boy!" She slinked from behind the counter and sashayed across the floor.

Kyla collapsed against a bolt of material with gales of laughter. When she finally regained a straight face, she allowed her thoughts to meander. "Maybe you're right, Madeline. I should do something positive. Like request that he come down here to do the photo layout for the portfolio."

"Of course I'm right. Go after what you want, in business or elsewhere."

Kyla continued with growing enthusiasm. "I could hire a few models and have them pose against some of the scenery right here—around Tubac! That way, my Southwest Indian clothing designs would be photographed in an authentic atmosphere, not in some studio. I can see them now! The traditional Navajo dress in yellow, with exquisite beadwork along the neckline and sleeves, displayed against the ancient Tumacacori Mission arches. A *manta* in white, with a side panel of brilliant embroidery, before the brown adobe ruins. And then there's the river and all the cottonwood trees around here that could make such attractive natural settings!"

Kyla's excitement mounted as her ideas multiplied. Her thoughts shifted from one very macho Griff Chansler to positive strategy for her first love, the new designing business. Thoughts of Griff, the man, were shoved to the background, as she considered all she had to do before this photo session took place. Then, Griff Chansler was only a vehicle through which she could implement her new endeavor. She was determined to get it the way she wanted it.

Madeline smiled eagerly. "Kyla, I think you're on to something! It sounds fabulous!"

"Pasqual says this portfolio will be our best selling tool. It's very important that everything in it is portrayed beautifully and professionally."

"Yes, and with the right kind of portfolio, you may have more orders than you and your two part-time employees can fill! Why, you can sell a line to Goldwater's and Levy's and Diamond's, as well as to the Indian shops around town. Then it will be easy to expand to Phoenix and throughout the state. The next step, of course, is to the Santa Fe and Taos boutiques.

Soon you'll be selling throughout the Southwest and extending to the western coast of California! Then—"

"Whoa! Hold it!" Kyla laughed at her friend's enthusiasm. "Give me a chance to get a solid start, Madeline! Don't project too far ahead! Right now, I just want to sell here in a corner of your shop in Tubac. Then maybe expand to Tucson."

Madeline wiggled a crooked, crippled finger at Kyla. "Don't think too small, young lady. Tubac is not a large-enough market for your business. It's fine for someone like me. But you? Why, Kyla, you have a gold mine of an idea here, with your original Southwest Indian styles of distinction. You'd better take advantage of it."

"Yes, Madeline," Kyla mocked in a subdued manner. "But, if I get too busy, how am I going to enjoy this beautiful new country I've fallen in love with? There'll be no time. I may as well go back to Chicago to do my designs and live in a skyscraper."

"Nonsense," Madeline scoffed. "You can have both success and freedom. If that's what you want."

"Oh, it is. Success and freedom." Kyla mulled over the words. "Sounds too good to be true! I just have to work at it. First, I need to check on my new employees. We have lots of clothes to make before I call Mr. Chansler about the portfolio. Later this week, I'm going to the Yaqui pre-Easter ceremonies. I especially want to see the Deer Dancer. Plus, I might pick up some fresh designs to use."

Madeline wrinkled her nose. "I've seen the Yaqui dances, and their costumes aren't as dramatic as the Pueblos and Hopi that you've seen."

"Well, you never know." Kyla didn't want to miss a

chance to see an Indian ceremonial. She felt a growing interest in the ancient rituals.

"Thanks for helping me with this fabric shipment, Kyla. There are some things around here I just can't handle with these clumsy hands."

Kyla gave her friend a quick hug around the shoulders. "That's what I'm here for, Madeline. And please call on me any time you need help. It's always my pleasure to help you." They were two women of different generations who happened to share ideas and work and the oneness of being female. Their friendship spanned the years that separated them, binding them together, ignoring the generation gap in between. It was a fun-loving, generous relationship with each grateful for the other, perhaps because each continued to be a changing, growing woman.

Halting, with her hand on the door, Kyla smiled mischievously, her dark eyes dancing with highlights, "Incidentally, it'll be interesting to see how Griff Chansler handles two aggressive women like us!"

Madeline laughed aloud, joining in Kyla's lively sparkle. "The man doesn't stand a chance!"

Kyla gazed, transfixed, at the lean, brown figure of the Deer Dancer. He was bare-chested, wearing only a skirtlike costume around his lower torso, and moved in rapid, tense motions, imitating the animal which the dance honored. The Yaqui fiesta dances, a strange combination of native and Catholic rituals, had continued for hours until, late in the night, the Deer Dancer made his spectacular appearance.

Kyla's attention was diverted momentarily by a motion in the small crowd. She turned her attention away from the dancer with antlers attached to his white-scarfed head and glimpsed a tall, Stetsoned cowboy, obviously a non-Indian. Kyla drew in her breath sharply as she faced Griff Chansler!

"Why, hello, Griff. Imagine meeting you in a place like this at this time of night!" She smiled a little shakily, her earlier arrogant confidence fleeing fast.

His hand touched the rim of his hat, greeting her cowboy style. "Hello, Kyla. Nice to see you again. I could say the same. What are you doing here? Taking more photos?" There was a touch of sarcasm in his voice.

"No," she admitted. "I just came to see the Yaqui Easter dances that I've heard so much about. And, of course, the Deer Dancer. No photos, though. I even left my camera at home."

"Good. At least you're staying out of trouble."

She angled her head his way and snapped, "I don't have to worry about that now that you've arrived! You're so handy at rescuing me from the Indians!"

"I'm not here to keep you straight!" he replied quickly.

"Oh? Since I'm one of your new clients, I thought you would want to make sure I stay out of trouble so my business will make money for you!"

"Frankly, Ms. Tramontano, I don't give a damn what happens to your business!" Griff's sharp words constricted in his throat. Of course he cared. She was, as she said, his client, and ordinarily he would never speak so harshly to a client. But these weren't ordinary circumstances, and this woman was anything but ordinary.

Yet, she was persistent and met his wrath with her

own sharp tongue. "Well, you'd better care, Mr. Chansler," she replied undaunted, "because if my business fails, your good name in the business community will go down with it! I'll see to that."

"My business was flourishing before you came along, and will not be affected one iota by the success or failure of yours!" He moved a step closer so they stood face to face in the firelight. Kyla could hear his sharp uptake of breath and feel his warm energy radiating in the cool of the night.

Suddenly, a dark shadow intervened between them, blocking the heat from the open fire. The Indian's voice was low and demanding. "Quiet! You will take this conversation somewhere else."

Griff's response to the Indian man was immediately apologetic. "Sorry. We . . . we just forgot." He took Kyla's elbow and steered her to the edge of the parking lot, effectively removing both of them from the Indians' dark glares. "Now, see here, Ms. Tramontano, once again you've managed to drag me into your quagmire. Don't you ever learn? You can't keep offending these people!"

"Me? I was standing there very quietly, minding my own business, until you appeared on the scene!"

"Minding your own business? I thought that was my job! You just accused me of it!"

"And a damn poor job you're doing of it, too!" she lashed out angrily. "The first thing you do is pawn me off on Pasqual because you can't deal with a woman who's in charge of her own affairs!"

"What?" he sputtered. "What in hell are you talking about?"

Kyla folded her arms across her chest, shivering a

little in the cool of the night. "I know the reason for your tactics. You can't stand a female who's assertive and enterprising!"

Griff seemed to rise even taller in his Western boots. "No, it's not the assertive female I mind! It's a woman who is aggressive and argumentative and obnoxious that infuriates me!"

"Obnox—" She choked on the word. No one had ever called her that! Cool and refined were words that described Kyla Tramontano. She had never been argumentative and obnoxious! Was she now? "I—I am not!" she protested in an unsophisticated reaction to his unfounded charges.

"You've apparently never experienced the assertiveness of a *real* man!"

Kyla smirked. "Is that why you won't work with me? Or is it because your fragile male ego won't tolerate a self-confident female?"

"Fragile male ego? I guarantee I can tolerate anything someone like you could dish out!" Whatever had made him think of her as vulnerable? Tender as a wild fawn? Why, this black-haired, black-eyed woman was a she-cat!

"Then why won't you take the photographs for my portfolio?"

"I could if—"

"Good. I want them taken in Tubac. Give me a week to get my designs together, then I'll expect you to handle my portfolio." Kyla wheeled on her heel, satisfaction hidden in a smug grin. Mission accomplished!

She hiked the short distance to her car, unlocked the door, and heaved herself angrily into the front seat. Taking a deep breath, she tried to calm her shaken nerves. The man was impossible! Obnoxious! That was a word that effectively described him, not her! Offensive was another way of describing Griff Chansler. He had used strong words as weapons against her. And they certainly had succeeded in riling her. Damn good, too!

She twisted the key and started her old, gray Chevy. As she wove her way out of the parking lot, Kyla slowly began to cool off from the heated argument with Griff. The pleasure of winning the confrontation was soured by the thought of facing him again. Would she be able to work with him on her precious portfolio? She'd probably be better off with Pasqual, after all.

Kyla glanced to the side of the road where a pickup truck was stalled. The hood was up and half of a male body dangled over the fender. Suddenly a stream of water shot straight up in the air and the body, belonging to one Griff Chansler, jumped away with the speed and grace of a frog. A bullfrog, at that! Kyla smothered a giggle as she watched the man's antics. She was tempted to gun the accelerator. But, for some reason, she didn't.

She just couldn't resist. "Need any help? You look pretty steamed."

He eyed her speculatively. "Matter of fact, I'm burning up! Are you offering to help?"

She shrugged. "I'll do whatever I can."

He lifted a dangling strip of rubber, obviously something that was broken. "Got any extra water?"

She shook her head.

"How about hose of any kind?"

"Nope. How about a ride into town? That's the best I can do."

He looked at his ailing truck, then back at her. She knew he was evaluating the offer. With the feathers flying so furiously between them only minutes ago, she thought it would dent his male ego to have to accept anything from her. "I suppose so. Let me cool this engine down first."

"Don't feel like you have to accept, Griff. It won't hurt my feelings a bit if you refuse. It's quite a long walk back to Tucson, but I'm sure one of your Indian friends will take time out from their Easter ceremony to give you a lift." It was an impossible statement, meant to dig him even deeper.

"Don't be such a wise ass. You know they won't leave the dance," he snarled. "Give me a few minutes to cool the engine down and lock my truck." When the water stopped gurgling from the engine, he slammed the hood and stalked around to the cab. Griff crawled into her car holding a camera.

"Oh, I hope you didn't plan to take any pictures tonight. I'm not sure I could handle more trouble from the Indians," she said breezily.

"I've already taken my photos tonight," he informed her and folded long legs into the cramped passenger area.

When she looked inquisitively at him, Griff explained curtly, "Special permission from my Indian friends."

Kyla burned with curiosity to ask him why he was able to obtain special permission and how one went about doing that. And what was he working on that was important enough to make the Indians waive their rules regarding the highly offensive photos? That would explain why he had appeared so coincidentally at two different Indian dances. Even locals didn't frequent the dances unless they had a special reason. But rather than quiz him about all those things, Kyla'd steam a hole in the seat first. She gunned the accelerator instead.

"Having car trouble is an old ruse, you know," she offered as they reached the highway.

"So is your offer of a lift. You could have driven on past me."

"Believe me, I considered it!"

"Well, why didn't you?"

"Not good for business. I just signed with your company this week. And maybe my conscience is working overtime."

"Figures. That's the capitalist in you, Kyla."

"Meeting head on with the capitalist in you, Griff."

"Are we back on a first-name basis again?" He shifted and his knee grazed hers.

"Looks like it. Actually, it'll be easier, since we're going to be working together. Mr. Chansler and Ms. Tramontano sounds awfully stuffy." They rode in silence until she turned off the highway again.

"Where are you taking me?"

He probably didn't realize how naive that sounded, she mused. "Where have I heard that line before?" she quipped, unable to avoid her sarcasm. "Don't worry, Griff. I'll get you home safe and sound."

"Home is not this way," he grumbled.

"My home is. I want you to meet a friend of mine. If you're going to be working in Tubac with me, you'll be seeing a lot of Madeline, too."

"Is she associated with your company?"

"She's mainly responsible for it. Madeline's a designer, too. We worked together in Chicago. She's very talented and creative and has been a teacher and friend to me. Now, with her encouragement and backing, I'm trying it on my own."

"She sounds interesting. And she must be enthusiastic about your work if she's willing to sink money into it."

"Not only that, she is a very special lady. That's why I want you to meet her."

There were obvious questions that crossed Griff's mind as Kyla drove behind the row of shops in Tubac and pulled into her driveway. Why did she really want him to meet Madeline? After the harsh words they'd exchanged, could they actually work together? Maybe this Madeline would be their go-between. Sounded reasonable.

Little did Griff know that the hidden agenda behind Kyla's action was actually the scrutiny of him by two conniving, assertive women!

Kyla showed him in the back door, which led directly into the kitchen. "Let me put some coffee on, then I'll get Madeline. She just lives next door. Please, have a seat, Griff."

He sat at the roughhewn table and gazed around the sparse kitchen. It was not as elegant as he would have expected for someone like Kyla. Apparently she was functioning on a bare-bones budget to get this business started. Kyla primed the coffeepot, then departed, leaving him alone to speculate. The rich aroma of coffee brewing arrested his senses, and Griff was filling his mug when the two women arrived.

"Ah, pouring your own coffee?" Kyla fizzed. "So you can be self-sufficient, after all. Or are you taking over my house?"

"Not only can I be, but I am very self-sufficient," he grated. "And I have no intention of taking over your house. But I am making myself comfortable."

She sniffed but forced a smile. "I want you to meet my dear friend, Madeline Vidal. Madeline, this is Griff Chansler." She had to catch herself to keep from saying *the* Griff Chansler.

They smiled formally and eyes met with instant affinity. It would have been obvious even to the casual observer. Griff extended his hand and Madeline immediately reciprocated, something she never did anymore. She usually protected her tormented hands like gold. But her first comment caught him short. "Don't squeeze, Griff. I don't care to know what a strong grip you have."

Instinctively, he looked at their hands, her crippled one resting so trustingly in his large mitt. "Madeline, I hope I didn't hurt you." He apologized quickly.

"Of course not. And I shouldn't have put you in such a position. I just couldn't help myself. I wanted to shake your hand." She smiled, and Griff clearly was impressed.

"Please sit down, Madeline. I'll get your coffee. Do you take anything in it? You, Kyla?" He proceeded to serve them both, proving how very self-sufficient he could be, even in Kyla's kitchen.

"Just cream," Madeline responded.

"Black." Kyla sat at the end of the table, allowing Madeline and Griff to sit across from each other.

"I'm sorry to bother you so late, Madeline. I was

stranded at the Reservation when my water hose burst. Fortunately, Kyla was there to rescue me. It was her idea to stop here tonight."

"Yes." Madeline smiled tolerantly. "Things usually are Kyla's idea. She knows I stay up late. I'm glad you stopped. I've been wanting to meet you, Griff."

"I understand you worked with Kyla back in Chicago," he said.

"Yes. We were both designers for a large clothes manufacturer. The work wasn't very creative. We usually designed exactly what we were told. But it was an excellent training ground."

Kyla inserted with a smile, "Most of the training came from Madeline. She is fabulous! She has designed for several of the major houses in New York and worked in Europe for a while."

"I'm impressed!" Griff said. "And now, you're retired in Tubac?"

"Retired?" roared Madeline. "Heavens no! I run my own material shop, specializing in hand-dyed and hand-printed material. My newest endeavor is a line of hand-dyed, Navajo yarn. I'll admit things were pretty quiet in Tubac until Kyla appeared on the scene. Now I'm involved with this wonderful, new design business of hers, and there aren't enough hours in the day! But I love it!"

"I can tell. So, Kyla has spiced up your life?" While Madeline talked enthusiastically about her new ventures, Griff reflected that, even though he had known Kyla only a few days, she had spiced up his life, too. And here he was, sitting in her kitchen, drinking coffee and chatting like an old friend, feeling right at home, and loving it.

When Madeline said good night, the hour was late, indeed. Griff walked her home, then returned to the inviting warmth of Kyla's kitchen. As he walked in the door, Kyla approached him with a grateful smile. She placed a hand on his arm and, tiptoeing, kissed him exactly on the lips.

To say that Griff Chansler was surprised would be an understatement. His mouth dropped slightly and every sinew in his body suddenly ached to ravish her. But he stood stock-still and said the first thing that popped into his head. "You are the damnedest, most aggressive female I've ever met!"

Her lips were still very close to his. "I wanted to thank you for being so wonderful with Madeline. Listening. Responding so positively to her. You made her feel like a woman tonight. That's very important, Griff."

"She's an amazing woman." His brown eyes were mesmerized by the aggressive young woman before him.

"Also, I wanted to see what it would feel like to kiss you. I've thought about it a long time. . . ." Kyla felt her throat closing up and wondered if it was possible to choke to death over a simple kiss.

"And . . . ?"

"Nice touch . . ." Kyla replied after a moment's consideration.

"I've never known a woman like you," Griff declared, shaking his head.

"You've never had a woman kiss you?" she asked incredulously. How long could they stand here like this, close enough to hear each other breathing, yet not touching?

"I've never had a woman make the first move before!"

"That's too bad. You've been missing out!" She stepped back, as if to move away.

Suddenly, Griff's powerful hands grasped her forearms, whipping her around to face him. "You want to know what it's like to kiss me, Kyla? That wasn't anything!"

His lips touched hers with virile ferocity. Griff's ego was definitely intact as he overpowered her, locking their lips in a scorching blast of fire. She would never forget what it felt like to kiss Griff.

CHAPTER FOUR

Their lips blended, feeling, exploring, delighting in the male-female difference they found.

Griff's lips moved aggressively over hers, revealing his masculine power. This kiss wasn't just a gentle touch, as Kyla's had been. It was more like staking a claim! A celebration of the senses! Even if his arms hadn't gripped her, Kyla couldn't have moved away. Not for a breath-gathering moment, anyway. He was inescapable! And so desirable! He tasted vaguely of mint, fresh and sweet. Kyla gasped at his strength, inhaling his masculine flavor as his lips continued their assault on her senses with no sign of stopping. She opened her mouth, tentatively at first, as Griff's tongue tantalized the sensitive inner circle of her lips.

Griff found Kyla's lips pliable, even under his force, and not fighting his dominance at all. She was smooth satin beneath his rough corduroy and he wanted to take her, have her completely. Now! He yearned to touch all of her, to feel that satiny, fawn-colored skin against him. Forcing her against his rock-hard frame, his hands slid down her back, resolutely molding her soft curves to his entire insatiable length. He felt her breasts press against his chest, as yielding and responsive as her lips. God! How he wanted to see them, touch them.

Without resistance, Kyla's arms reached up to circle Griff's broad shoulders. She clung, breathlessly, amazed at her reaction to this man's kiss. Only one kiss! And all she wanted was more of him! She wanted to feel his hard muscles against her, to press him to her, to know his strength. Willingly, she succumbed to the magic that swept over them both, wrapping, swirling, besieging.

Griff realized her compliance to his desires and eased up on the amount of force he exerted to keep her against him. She was there of her own will, her desires merging with his own. Now, his lips were persuasive, not forceful; enticing, not coercive. His hands caressed her back, tracing her spine through the thin material of her shirt. One hand sought her rounded buttocks, pressing her to his loins so she could feel what she did to him. They were spontaneous electricity together.

Kyla opened her lips to his gentle probing, marveling at the pungent taste of him, loving the sensations that radiated through her. She touched his compelling tongue with her own, motivating his increased passion. She was every ounce a woman, swept unavoidably into the aura of Griff's masculinity. And she wanted it to continue its natural course until they were one together. Griff's hands caressed her back, reaching for her hips, forcing her to him with ever-increasing strength. His masculine hardness buttressed between them, and he moved persuasively against her, stimulating them both.

Griff's tongue plunged to the depths, claiming her with a definite rhythm and strength. Kyla moaned in response to his sudden power, wanting to succumb, knowing she must resist. Soon there would be no stopping!

With unquenched aching in every part of her, Kyla struggled for control. Her hands dropped to his chest and pushed weakly. It was an elementary act, but this turbulence had to stop! What was she doing? One kiss and they were both aroused! Ready to take a chance! Oh, no! Not again! She hardly knew him, and he wasn't even her type of man!

"Griff—" It was a hoarse sound of protest.

"You're intoxicating, Kyla—" he rasped, his voice stormy with unchecked passion. It made him all the more virile and appealing.

His grip loosened from her back, and Kyla writhed from his arms, from his heated body. "Griff, I—"

"My God, Kyla. I don't know what happened!"

She smiled faintly at his innocent avowal. "I do! And I'm sure you could figure it out, too."

Even with her teasing, he remained serious. "Well, it shouldn't have happened. I lost control. We both did."

"That was some kiss," she admitted, pushing back a wisp of long, dark hair that had struggled loose from its moorings.

Instinctively, Griff's hand reached out to caress her coal-black mane. "That was some response."

Suddenly, she felt weak and needed to lean on something. Someone strong. "I'll say! Too . . . too much.

I didn't mean to do that. Didn't mean for that to happen, Griff."

He kept his hand on her, stroking her hair until long, masculine fingers rested sensuously around the back of her neck. "Neither did I. But, I'm not denying what you do to me, Kyla. There's something special between us. Electricity!"

She froze at his touch, her eyes beseeching his. *What was he saying?* They'd been battling only a few short hours ago. Fire from his fingertips radiated down her back and resurging feelings of feminine desire spread through her. Kyla, a strong and assertive, totally self-possessed female, was overwhelmed with the longing to yield to Griff's masculinity. "Griff . . . will you . . . hold me? Just for a minute . . ."

Suddenly she was vulnerable, someone who needed him. With a small, groaning sigh, he enfolded her with long, strong arms, holding her against the security of his warm body. "Oh yes . . . yes, Kyla . . . you can't fight this forever . . . hmmm, you smell nice . . ." His lips melted soft kisses on her neck, branding her with slow desire that spread through her.

Kyla inhaled his pungent, masculine aroma and felt his heart pulsating with vigor. She wrapped her arms tightly around his middle, a child clutching for love, a vulnerable woman seeking her heart's desire.

In that beautiful moment of holding and sharing, Griff knew his earlier instincts about this woman had been correct. Vulnerable. Kyla was a strong woman and had an even stronger facade. But beneath that crusty she-cat was a sensitive woman. A soft, vulnerable woman who needed him. *Oh, my God, what am I thinking? I have nothing to give anyone!*

Griff could not, would not, let that happen again. Oh yes, he would take her feminine pleasures, if offered. He would even provide masculine strength and physical satisfaction. He could enjoy her company. But he would never give completely of himself. The ultimate price was too high.

She stirred against his chest. "Griff, I . . . I'm sorry."

"Sorry? Don't be." He wasn't ready for her to leave him. Not yet.

Kyla moved again, this time departing from the warm security of his arms. She moved clumsily to the kitchen cabinet and poured more coffee for them both. "I didn't intend for any of this to happen, Griff. That's not why I brought you here tonight."

He accepted the coffee from her, their warm hands touching in the process. "Why did you bring me here?" he challenged. What was she doing? Testing him?

She sighed, not looking at him, now somewhat chagrined at what had transpired between them so suddenly. "I wanted you to meet Madeline. That was an honest effort. No," Kyla amended slowly. "Actually, I wanted her to meet you. Madeline was curious about Chansler Marketing and what it can do for my business. Mostly, though, I wanted you to see my operation here. I needed your opinion . . . maybe your endorsement. This is new for me. I feel like a neophyte."

A faint, crooked smile began to form. "You don't feel like a neophyte to me."

"I am," she affirmed, lifting her face. "In the business world."

"Now, let's see," Griff began with amusement. "You brought me to your home to show me your etchings? Wonderful! I've always wanted to do that."

"I could show you my sketches," she added to his bantering with a small smile, glad for a little humor between them. "The designs are in the other room."

"So, show me."

"My operations aren't very elaborate now. Believe it or not, we're working in the front room of this house." Kyla led the way through the narrow, plastered hallway.

Griff followed, observing the proud lines of her back and the nice motion of her slim hips. Her flowing stride caught his attention and, once again, he was reminded of his first glimpse of the woman in the backless sundress and violet glasses. *Nice back. Nice legs. Soft, full breasts!*

Politely, Griff examined her materials, the designs she had in stock, the sketches for future fashions. They discussed her ideas for the layout photos and his choices of the designs that would show up best. By the time they finished, it was well past midnight.

"Kyla, I'm very impressed with your 'operation,' as you call it. I agree with Madeline. You have a winning idea here, and I'm very enthusiastic about your designs. You're going to make it. With or without Chansler Marketing."

"Thanks for your comments and your confidence, Griff. But I need your help. Marketing is important, and it's not my field. It's yours. Your advice is valuable."

"You already have a remarkable insight into the retailing business. Marketing comes next."

"Can I confess something? There was another reason that I invited you here tonight, Griff." She turned away from his brown-eyed gaze, now embarrassed by her deviousness.

"Oh? Do I detect some feminine scheming?" His tone was teasing, and he ran a finger a short distance up her forearm, enough to stir her senses.

"You might say that," she admitted softly. "I wanted to evaluate you."

Surprisingly, he laughed. "Evaluate me? Why? Is that why you brought Madeline into the picture?"

"I highly regard Madeline's opinions. It just seemed important to know more about the man who would be guiding my business." She bent her head, feeling like a traitor. "You must understand that because I'm new out here, I don't know who I can trust."

He folded his arms and prodded. "I'm curious. What's my rating?"

She answered reluctantly. "High. Very high. Maybe, too . . ."

"What about trusting? Do you trust me?"

"I'm really confused. I didn't intend for this . . . this to happen . . . between us." She groped futilely for words. "I don't know if it was my fault or yours."

"Kyla." His voice was low and his hands gripped her arms lightly. "Believe me, the kiss wasn't planned. But I don't regret it and hope you don't either. Incidentally, you can trust me."

"In what way?"

He stiffened. "You can trust me as a business associate. Our personal relationship will be up to you. I won't force anything between us." He would make no promises to this woman who made his blood run hot and cold at the same time. She scared him and excited him. One kiss, and he knew. *But, no promises, little she-cat.*

"I believe you, Griff," she answered without hesitation. "I like . . . what I see."

He kissed her nape, once, twice . . . and a shiver ran through her. "You're the damnedest, most honest woman I've ever met."

She turned toward him, a satisfied smile on her lips. "Then you're not turned off by my . . . honesty? Or my aggressiveness?"

"Not at all. I like it. And I like what I see, too."

She reached up, hands resting tentatively on his chest. "Griff, can I . . . touch your hair? It's so . . . beautiful, I've wanted to touch it since that day in your office when I first saw its color."

He laughed delightedly, from deep in his chest. "I've never heard that before! Of course, you can touch anything you like!"

First, her hand smoothed over the top of his deep auburn hair. She felt its waves, stroked its rough texture. "Griff! Do you mean that no woman has ever asked to run her fingers through your hair? Why, it's like . . . deep burgundy . . ." Her long fingers dug into the thickness, scraping roughly along his scalp, stretching around to the back.

With a low groan, Griff's head lowered to hers, his lips capturing hers in a kiss that couldn't be resisted. Without waiting for an invitation this time, his tongue ravaged deep into her mouth, taking her breath. Kyla clung to him, pressing her head against his, retaining the hypnotic force of the kiss.

Vaguely, she knew she was propelled against his

virile body, knew his hands caressed the length of her, knew the masculine strength that held her firmly. His tongue dipped in sensuous motions in her mouth and she responded, all too positively. Almost immediately, he stopped the powerful thrusting and swept her up in his arms, holding her easily against his pounding chest.

"Where is your bedroom?" It was a rough demand.

"I . . . Griff, no—I think I'd better take you home."

"I don't want to go home. I want you—"

She didn't let him finish. "Please, Griff. Put me down. I . . . this is not right! I can't!"

He plunked her to the floor, letting her feet fall with a thud. "What the hell? First you lure me here. Then you kiss me—first, mind you! Then you tempt me and taunt me all evening, admitting you like certain things, showing me your etchings . . ."

"Sketchings."

". . . then apologizing innocently, then running your fingers through my hair, then . . . you tell me no! What do you think I'm made of . . . steel?"

"Griff, I . . . I'm sorry. No, I don't think you're made of steel. I think I like you very much. Too much. And, too fast. I just need some time. You do, too."

"I'll take all the time you need. Tonight!"

"Not tonight. I think I'd better take you home now," she suggested weakly.

"At this time of night? Are you crazy? If you spend an hour driving me home, then you'd be on the road, by yourself, after two A.M.! No way!"

She grinned. "I'm a big girl. I can take care of myself. Being on the road at night doesn't bother me."

"Well, it's unsafe. The idea's a poor one. I guess I'm too macho to agree to it!"

Kyla laughed as he used her very word to describe himself. Perhaps he was. And perhaps that's what she liked so much about him. "Well, looks like we have no alternative."

"Oh yes, there are alternatives," he explained patiently. "If you take me home, you'll have to spend the night, because I won't let you return at this time of night on the highway alone."

"Won't let me?" she chortled with disdain. It had been a long time since a man declared he wouldn't *let* her do something. And, even longer since she had paid attention to that demand, much less obeyed!

"Yes. I won't let you come back alone. I'll take good care of you at my house. Separate beds, I promise."

She laughed at his promise. "Oh, yes?"

"Sure. Don't you trust me?"

"No!" she exclaimed.

"Smart girl," he cracked. "Another alternative is that I simply spend the brief remainder of the night here, and you take me back to Tucson in the light of day. If we choose that one, there is no way you can keep your local friends and neighbors from knowing that a man spent the night with you, in this tiny house. It wouldn't matter where we slept. They would make their own deductions. At this point, it might not be too good for your new business."

She shook her head negatively. "I don't like that idea. Normally, I wouldn't care what anyone thought. But you're probably right about my new business here. And people in small communities do gossip terribly. Anyway, I don't have a spare bedroom."

"Then, there's the third, dull, unimaginative idea. I could just take your car and drive myself home. But we'd be stuck with getting it back down here to you."

"Dull and unimaginative or not, it seems the best solution. Why don't you just go ahead and take my car? You can return it first thing tomorrow morning," she offered. "But make it early because I need the car to pick up a new stock shipment for Madeline. And I need to do some shopping in Tucson."

"This simple situation is getting very complicated, you know," he droned, feigning crabbiness. "I have an appointment with an important client at the office tomorrow morning."

"So, looks like we both need a car in the morning," she pondered.

"Back to square one. And the first solution. I liked it best, anyway. Get your coat and toothbrush," he ordered brusquely.

"Griff! I don't want to spend the night with you!"

"Separate beds, remember? Come on. Don't be such a stiff-neck! You're the one who ran fingers through my hair, you sexy wench! And I didn't even get to reciprocate! Now, let's see how modern you really are!"

Within minutes, Kyla and Griff were speeding along the highway, heading north. Kyla wondered if she was actually modern enough to pull this off, with no regrets. Changing woman? Well, she hadn't changed that much! And Griff? Would he stay out of her bed, given the circumstances? He was, after all, a lusty, virile man. And she? A lusty, sexy woman! She *had* kissed him first! And then had responded eagerly to his kisses.

Countering those thoughts was another niggling question: Did she want him to avoid her? She was, admittedly, attracted to him. Kyla glanced at Griff, who had assumed the traditional male role of driver, even though it was her car.

Due to the late hour and lack of traffic, it took less than an hour to reach Tucson. The first thing Kyla noticed as they pulled into the driveway of Griff's foothills home was the black Jaguar. It was sleek and beautiful. Next to it was parked a light blue Volvo station wagon.

"Well, you should be able to get wherever you're going tomorrow," she cracked. "Here you are with two expensive vehicles, and you're relying on my old gray Chevy!"

"Hmmm," he agreed. "They don't make them the way they used to. Sometimes the oldest are the most reliable."

"I'd say that was true for most things."

"Maybe you're right." Griff steered her into the house from the rear, which was rather plain with a small garden for the entranceway. But, once inside, the house opened up with sliding glass doors and ample windows that overlooked a huge, tiled pool, then the city lights. The view was spectacular!

"Oh, Griff, it's beautiful!" Kyla glided to one of the doors and out onto the veranda before she realized it. The pool shimmered with blue and yellow Italian tile and reflected the multicolored lights from the city of Tucson.

"Would you like to take a swim tonight?" His hand rested on her shoulder.

Oh my, it was inviting! Kyla quivered inside with

the urge to say "yes," but shook her head. "I didn't bring—" Suddenly she realized that Griff knew she didn't bring a thing, except her toothbrush. And it certainly wasn't necessary to wear a swimsuit in a moonlit pool with this much privacy!

His voice rumbled low and inviting. "It's excellent at night. So cool and refreshing. You should try it."

She shook her head again, more strongly this time. "I'm really very tired, Griff. I think I'd better go to bed. And you, too, if you have an early appointment."

"I thought you'd never ask," he chuckled, leading her back into the house.

"I didn't suggest—" She followed him, wondering if she could fight him off should he force himself on her. Wondering if she would try . . .

"Here is the guest bedroom. The bath is adjoining. There should be plenty of towels. Make yourself at home." He was abrupt, almost curt. He turned, then stopped and looked at her. "You haven't changed your mind?"

Kyla looked at him perceptively and stubbornly shook her head. He wanted her. It was obvious in his every movement, his unspoken words. And, she wanted him, too. Her eyes betrayed the desire, even while she shook her head "no."

Griff wheeled, without another word, and closed the door behind him.

Kyla looked around the room, her gaze falling on the bed. She was tired and the bed looked welcoming. She brushed her teeth and stripped off her jeans and shirt. Drawn to the window for one more glimpse of the view outside, she pulled her curtain aside. The entire valley in which the city of Tucson nestled twinkled with a million colored lights. The pool, luminescent and quivering, reflected those lights invitingly.

A delightful thought began to form in her tired mind, an idea that was exciting and mischievous. It was not exactly forbidden, yet she had refused the invitation to do it earlier. But why not now? Alone and quiet. It would be so exhilarating! And refreshing! And relaxing! She listened and heard nothing. She was sure Griff had already gone to bed.

With the stealth of a mountain cat, Kyla slipped her towel-wrapped, nude body into the hallway. She listened again. Nothing. Her heart pounded beneath the hand that clutched the towel to her breasts. She was a child, slipping out of the house, a burglar stealing a moment of glory! She crossed the brick veranda and moved, magnetized, to that shimmering, glimmering pool. The water was absolutely gorgeous and inviting! Kyla dropped the towel, feeling very assured that she was alone. Just she and the pool and the lights in the distance below.

Kyla did not see the tall, dark figure at the far end of the veranda by the pool. The only indication of another's presence was a faint red glow from a cigarette that moved occasionally. Ominous, dark, masculine eyes stalked her with animal ease and fascination. He was lying in ambush. Kyla was a she-cat, lured into his snare.

With the first step, cool water flurried around her ankles and she gasped audibly. The water was colder than she expected. Isn't it always? she mused and proceeded down the steps. She entered slowly, too slowly, allowing the water to inch up her body. A silvery chill edged up her long legs, sending shivers reverberating through her by the time it reached upward for her thighs. When the icy water lapped at her bottom, she could stand it no longer and dove in, taking half the length of the pool underwater. It was every bit as wonderful and exhilarating as she imagined it would be, and Kyla methodically lapped the pool twice, stroking freestyle.

It was when she stopped to catch her breath that she realized she wasn't alone!

Griff stood at the edge of the pool, provocative, indomitable . . . completely nude. His dark eyes caught hers electrically for a fleeting moment before his sleek body dove into the water, aiming for her like a missile.

Mesmerized, and with feminine appreciation, Kyla watched his exacting male form slice through the water. His long, outstretched arms realigned the muscles in his back; his waist tapered, then formed tight buttocks; his legs extended and kicked slightly to speed his voyage. She tread water, anticipating his emergence near her. From the moment she gazed up at his figure on the edge of the pool, aroused and formidable, Kyla knew she would be in Griff's arms tonight. It was inevitable, and she waited with growing expectation.

"You didn't think I would let you enjoy this alone," he chided as he emerged, water dripping sensuously down his face.

"I didn't think . . . you would be here."

"Oh, come on now. I'm not blind. I saw the way you looked at this pool. I knew you'd be back. You couldn't resist."

"Then you knew it before I did."

He shrugged. "Maybe so. There are some things you know, little she-cat. Like the certainty that I couldn't resist you. It was inevitable from the first." His arms reached for her, pulling her slick form to his.

Although her flesh was willing, Kyla objected weakly. "Griff, I don't think we should—" His overwhelming virility, so close and breathtaking, stopped further protestations.

The water whirled around them, squishing around her breasts until they were pressed tight against his chest and there was no more room for anything between them. Nothing but throbbing hearts and tingling flesh could keep them apart. His lips sought hers, and Kyla clutched his shoulders, bracing on him to stay above the water. Their lips melded, as if they belonged together, no hesitation from either side. The kiss lasted long after their blended forms drifted below the surface of the glittering water. It was heaven as they swirled together, touching, enjoying, finally shooting to the surface gasping for air.

They laughed and played, chasing, dunking, drawing together for tempting kisses, then falling away to backstroke across the waves. Hands cavorted playfully, touched curiously, stroking sensitively. Griff's body was long and solid and vigorous. Kyla was slim and pliant and responsive. Finally, they drew together because they could stay apart no longer. She wrapped her arms tightly around his muscular shoulders, grasping for his masculine warmth.

"I'm cold," Kyla murmured, shivering against him, entwining her long legs around his waist.

He quivered with the arduous yielding of her fawnlike skin to his, high with the promise of her feminine softness malleable with fervid passion, closing around him. With velvet lips pressed to her neck, he murmured, "We have to get out of the pool, Kyla. Then I'll warm you . . ."

He cupped his hands under her buttocks and carried her, the two of them dripping across tile and bricks and brilliant rugs. When they reached the bedroom, both experienced the peaks of expectation as they writhed exuberantly, passionately together. Suddenly waiting became impossible, and with her legs still wrapped around his middle, Griff lowered her onto his throbbing masculinity. The world crashed around them in wild explosions, and Griff braced himself against the wall and held her securely against him.

"Hold on for a wild ride," he managed to gasp.

"Oh, Griff . . ." Kyla muffled into his shoulder, her teeth making small, agonizing marks as desire gripped her with feverish intensity.

"Come on, little she-cat! You're mine tonight!"

Kyla had never known such an immediate, passionate response to a man, had never experienced such wild abandon. She braced on his shoulders, unconsciously digging her fingernails into his sinews. She felt as though her entire body was floating, falling, erupting into a million blazing pieces! She was rent apart by his thrusting, but an ancient instinct made her arch against him, forcing him even further into her. Their climax was an exploding rage, simultaneous and furious. Then, quiet ecstasy. They were together, as one, breathless and exhausted. Finally satisfied. Fulfilled. Inebriated with overflowing ecstasy.

At last, Griff lowered her onto the bed, murmuring

soothing words, stroking and kissing her sensitive parts.

"That was a little too fast," he apologized gravely. "Was I . . . too rough?"

"I was a little rough, myself," she chuckled softly, caressing the marks on his shoulders with gentle fingers. "Did I hurt you?"

"That's supposed to be my line," he reprimanded gruffly. "You're a regular little hellion, Kyla. A real she-cat when you're aroused . . ." His hands encircled her back, pulling her fawn-colored skin against his.

She clung to Griff's warmth, his security. This masculinity that had attracted her from the beginning completely overpowered them both, and Kyla lay content in that knowledge and his arms. It restored her sense of self, her confidence in her femininity. She would be ever grateful to Griff Chansler for that. *Grateful? Is that why she agreed to this? So she could be grateful?* Kyla buried her face against his chest, embarrassed with the thought, wondering if she would be sorry when morning came. Right now, she only knew she was filled with longing for this man. Her marvelous, macho cowboy, Griff Chansler . . .

Before the night was over, they made love again, this time slowly and leisurely. Again, Kyla responded vigorously. She delighted in Griff's every touch and kiss, ached for his fulfillment long before he chose to culminate their passion in a frenzied storm. Lightning and thunder intensified their ardor, hurling them through the tempest, battering them savagely, leaving them drenched in the moisture of their own lovemaking.

Kyla nestled her head against Griff's arm, her lashes dark feathers on flushed cheeks. Her warm body cuddled close, drawing him to her tawny skin, pressing him to her rounded, relaxed breasts. He pulled the sheet and light blanket over them, thinking how beautiful and . . . vulnerable she looked in sleep.

The next morning, all was quiet, and Griff was gone when Kyla awoke. She stared around the strange room, then realized that she was in Griff's bed. She blinked at the brightness, forcing herself fully awake. It was late and she had work to do. She bounded out of his bed and made it up, smoothing the cover as if to hide any signs of their lovemaking.

She found her toothbrush and scrubbed three full minutes with it. Then Kyla took a quick shower, lathering her hair, and rinsing away all traces of a man from her body. She couldn't believe she had done such a thing. To go to bed with Griff Chansler was unsavory business practice. Oh, how could she face him now?

She toweled her hair and strolled through his house, admiring his taste, glancing at the telltale pool. She walked barefoot outside on the warm bricks and combed her ebony hair in the sunshine, drying it naturally. Back inside, she rummaged in his near-empty refrigerator and found a stalk of celery. Mentally she applauded him—a bachelor who stocked fresh vegetables in lieu of frozen TV dinners. It was then that she saw the note.

Scrawled in Griff's handwriting was *Coffee in cabinet above coffee maker. I'm late for my appt. Your fault, she-cat! I will see you again soon!* She smiled, in spite of her embarrassment. Now, why should she be chagrined? Griff was a fascinating and handsome man who had seduced her. She was only human! Or had she done the seducing? She had gone to bed with him willingly . . . perhaps too willingly! Nevertheless, he made fabulous love, and she had responded eagerly, and now, her heart sang with fulfillment.

Kyla decided to forgo the coffee. There was too much to do and she was late already. She stuffed the toothbrush into her purse and left Griff's foothills home in her dowdy gray Chevy. He had taken the sleek, black Jag.

After she ran errands and picked up the stock shipment for Madeline, Kyla headed southward for her lush, Santa Cruz Valley home. When she drove up to the simple adobe house, her two employees met her at the door, jibbering a rapid-fire combination of English and Spanish.

"Wait! Hold on! Tell me slowly!" she instructed firmly.

"Señorita Kyla, the man, he come. And he tear the place apart! Aiyee! What a mess!" Carmen wrung her hands.

"Man? What man? What was he doing?" The only man who came to her mind at the moment was Griff Chansler. Griff had been here this morning? It didn't make sense.

"The man," Ed Nah spoke calmly, interrupting the hysterical Carmen. "The man with the funny little beard came. He claimed you knew him, and demanded that we let him in. Then he tore the place apart and finally took the papers. He took all those sketches in the drawer!"

Kyla was dumbstruck. It had to be Ian! Damn! He

had found her! Now, just when she thought she was rid of him, he was back to torment her! Just when she had a new life going! And, did she dare admit, a new love?

CHAPTER FIVE

A week passed before Kyla heard from Griff again. It was just as well. She was frantic over Ian's burglary of her design sketches, and the knowledge that he had found her, even with her relocation and recent name change. She had thought he was securely exiled in California. It seemed so far away from Chicago, Kyla was sure she would never see him again. However, from Arizona, California was only a quick flight away. Suddenly she was frighteningly close to him . . . provided he was in California.

Each day was filled with fear that Ian would walk through the door, and Kyla took some extra security precautions. She didn't want her employees exposed to the terror of this bearded wildman from her past, so she installed a dead-bolt lock on the front door and gave Ed Nah and Carmen permission to enter and exit through the kitchen. Essentially, they locked themselves in to work. It left very little personal privacy for

Kyla, but she felt so strongly about forging her new business that she was willing to sacrifice almost anything in order to establish it. And they had to feel safe where they worked. The fact that Ian was again pursuing her designs emphasized her personal conviction that they were marketable and good. Damn good! Her self-esteem was again intact.

Kyla also established a different system for protecting her designs. The only things now stored in her desk were pencils and scraps of paper. The real sketches were kept in a kitchen drawer, under the plastic tray that held cooking utensils. It wasn't very sophisticated protection, but it was all she could afford at the time. Duplicate sketches were with Madeline, hidden somewhere, even from Kyla. They were dealing with a devious man, this Ian, and the two women prepared themselves for his return. Inevitably, he would.

It was a frightening thought to Kyla, especially since she knew what destruction he was capable of, both professionally and emotionally. She had been involved with him once, and it had been a disastrous mistake. He left her career ruined and her emotions wrecked. Would he return to produce the same devastation? Kyla cringed at the thought. No, she resolved. She wouldn't, just *couldn't,* let that happen. She was changing, growing, and she would never again be the same dependent woman Ian had manipulated.

Kyla spent the week working on replacing her sketches, trying to recall certain details that made her Desert Spirit designs so distinctive. There were changes, alterations, inevitable diversions from the originals that Ian had stolen. But Kyla knew she held the trump card that Ian couldn't possibly have. She had Ed Nah.

Ed Nah Trailing Flower had proven to be an unexpected jewel. She was a lovely Navajo woman who had grown up on the vast Navajo Reservation which straddled New Mexico and Arizona. Now she and her family made their home in Tucson. She came highly recommended, and Kyla hired her immediately because of her expert skills in doing authentic beadwork and cutout appliqués.

Given Ed Nah's life and experiences, it was only natural that she knew Indian designs. Genuine Indian designs! Furthermore, she was willing to share that knowledge with Kyla! She could see that Kyla's work was beautiful and distinctive. Now, with Ed Nah's input, Desert Spirits could produce authentic garments that perpetuated the beauty and art of native Americans. The new clothing line became as important to Ed Nah as it was to Kyla, and the two of them worked enthusiastically to produce it.

Already, Ed Nah had spent hours at the rustic kitchen table with Kyla and Madeline discussing styles, contributing to the designs, adding knowledge about significant symbols to be used in appliqués. With some training in basic design and textiles, Ed Nah could become a future designer, one of a team. She was fast becoming a valuable part of the organization. When Desert Spirits became established and grew large enough . . . when they expanded out of the humble adobe workroom . . . Kyla sighed with wishful anticipation and was snapped back to reality by the ringing of the phone.

"Is this the woman who enjoys midnight swims?" Griff's voice was low and sexy.

Kyla smiled instantly, unable to avoid the warm tingles that engulfed her when she recognized his voice. "Yes. Is this the man who uses a broken-down truck as a device to get picked up?"

"The same!" He laughed. "Are you ready to set up a time for the photography session. It seems I backed myself into that endeavor."

"Yep. You agreed. But I'm not quite ready to set it up, Griff. This week has been slower than expected." She wouldn't mention the problems created by Ian's unwelcomed visit. Not yet, anyway.

"Well, now. I'm looking for an excuse to see you again, Kyla. If you don't need me to photograph the portfolio, what ruse can I invent to come to Tubac? I could drive the truck by your house just in time to run out of gas. But you're wise to my tactics." He was so open and honest in his intentions, Kyla couldn't help laughing.

"I'll give you a legitimate reason," she offered generously. "How about lunch?"

"That's what I like. A woman with straightforward ideas. Lunch sounds great. Today?"

"Yes. There is a style show at the Tubac Valley Country Club today that I want to attend. I'll meet you in the bar of The Stables at twelve-thirty."

"Fine. I'll be there." Griff lowered the phone and winced, thinking, *A style show? Why in hell did I agree to that?* But he didn't stew long, for there was only one answer to the question. He could hardly wait to see her again.

The hour's drive south from Tucson to the small

artists' community of Tubac gave Griff time to think about this new woman in his life. She was, indeed, beautiful. Naturally, he would be attracted to her. However, from the first, even before he knew what she looked like, he was drawn to Kyla. It was a dangerous sign. He had purposely stayed away from her this week, fearing the indomitable attraction he felt toward her, and a possible repeat of his weak-willed action of that night by the pool.

Oh God, the sight of her nude, in the moonlight, was just too much. After all, he was only a man. Resisting her was beyond his reasoning. He would, however, curb himself next time he was around Kyla. *Control!* he repeated silently.

The roofs of the tiny, historic community of Tubac were barely visible from the busy highway that led from Tucson to the border town of Nogales. However, what wasn't apparent was the atmosphere and verdant coolness that infiltrated the beautiful area along Santa Cruz Valley. There was something special about the place, once entered, that created an energy, a feeling of deep appreciation for the glorious realm's endurance. Located on the Santa Cruz River, Tubac was an oasis of giant cottonwoods, poplars, and rich farmlands set amid a desert land that produced nothing taller than scrub oak.

Maybe the energy came from those who had inhabited the land in past eras. The valley's solitude had survived bloody battles from Yuma and Pima Indian revolts against Spanish invaders in the fifteenth century. In the 1700s missions and presidios attempted to protect settlers, only to be abandoned to the warring Apaches. In the 1800s an uneasy peace between conquering Spanish and fierce Apaches ended in an Indian massacre, destroying the entire Tubac settlement.

Modern archaeologists and curiosity-seekers still stumbled through the adobe ruins of these earlier inhabitants. It was hard to imagine this resplendent, peaceful valley strewn with blood and victims of war. Now it served as a haven for artists and others who wanted a departure from the pressures of the contemporary world. Tubac was a charming escape, and Griff could understand why Kyla had fallen in love with it.

A slight breeze ruffled Griff's deep auburn hair as he stepped onto the Tubac Country Club grounds. He glanced up at puffy white clouds, wondering if they purposely graced the Santa Cruz Valley with rain, keeping it green and productive, while ignoring the dry surrounding hills.

The old hacienda of the original land-grant ranch was used only sparingly, but the quaint ranch stables had been converted into a unique restaurant called, aptly enough, The Stables. Uneven rock floors, a huge fireplace, brick archways, even some of the original horse stalls remained a distinction of the decor.

When Griff arrived, Kyla was already there, perched sideways on one of the unique saddle barstools. He blinked in the darkness before discerning Kyla's shapely figure, her fingers toying with a napkin while she talked to the bartender. Those legs! That's what he noticed first, as her dress was hitched above her knees due to the way she had to sit on the saddle seat.

"Is this saddle taken?" Griff heaved a leg over the barstool next to Kyla and settled into the creaking leather.

Kyla smiled, a genuine glow lighting her face at the sight of Griff. "It's saved for a tall gentleman who likes Indian dances and midnight swims."

"I guess you've pegged me, Señorita. I'll fight any man who tries to knock me outta this saddle." He crossed his wrists on the saddle horn and drawled, "I've been a-ridin' the range all day, little lady, and my throat is as dry as a bleached bone lyin' in the dust. What have you got to wet my whistle? Sarsaparilla?"

"I was thinkin' of something a mite stronger, myself." She laughed, gesturing to the bartender. "Ricardo, here, tells me he makes the best margaritas this side of the border. Is that right, Ricardo?"

"*Sí*, Señorita," the bartender grinned.

"Then, let's try them," Griff agreed wholeheartedly. *"Dos margaritas, por favor."*

Kyla turned to him seriously. "I realize you have no interest in this style show, Griff. Actually, even I consider it strictly business. The show is being presented by a designer out of Taos, and it's very important for me to see what she has to offer." Her tone was almost apologetic. "Anyway, the food and atmosphere here are good. I hoped that would make up for you having to sit through a style show."

Griff's hand covered hers. "Don't you realize I wanted to see you again? I'll sit through anything to accomplish that. Anyway, watching women isn't such a bad way to spend the day."

She smiled tolerantly. "You sound like a cowpuncher who's been on the trail too long and away from the company of women."

He squeezed her hand and his warm touch added to

the lingering memories of their night together. "Nope. Just desperate for the company of one dark-haired lady."

"After we eat lunch, I'll take you to some of the places I'd like you to consider as a setting for the portfolio photos."

"Good. Apparently you already have a few places in mind." Griff fished a few dollars out of his pocket when the drinks arrived.

Ricardo shook his head. "They've already been paid for, Señor."

"Already paid—" Griff shot a glance at Kyla. "You?"

"Who else?" She laughed at his shocked expression. "This is my invitation and my treat."

"I'll be damned!"

"Well, so will I!" She couldn't help mocking him. "I've already told you this is a business luncheon, Griff. My business."

"You are the—"

She interrupted, placing her hand on his arm. "I know! I'm the damnedest, most aggressive female you've ever encountered!"

"Damn right! I can't even brandish my own expletives! You beat me to that, too!" He bristled. "Thank God there's one custom where I can exhibit my masculinity in an aggressive manner!"

"And you do exhibit your masculinity quite aggressively," she commented dryly.

"Is that a compliment?" he asked.

She nodded with a coy smile, not at all embarrassed by the turn of the conversation. "Extraordinary. Marvelous. Exemplary."

"Exemplary?" He kissed her earlobe and murmured, "God, you're gorgeous! Do we have to stay for this damned style show?"

"Yes. That's why we're here."

"That's why *you're* here," he amended.

"It's important for me to see it."

"And you're important to me. So, I guess I'll stay, hard as it may be." A look of agony crossed his face and he checked to see if she noticed.

Kyla loved his sexy teasing, but ignored his ribald insinuation. "Madeline and Wade will be meeting us soon. I think you'll like Wade. He's a retired engineer and, I'm sure, is tagging along today merely because Madeline asked him to accompany her. You two will probably have a lot in common."

"An engineer? I doubt it," Griff observed. "My field is marketing, remember?"

"And photography. How can I forget?" Kyla sipped her frosty drink.

"Not photography." He shook his head morosely. "I got rooked into that, on all counts."

"One thing you have in common with Wade is that you both think Madeline is terrific. I'll admit, I agree."

"Yes, that's true. I still think it's a little strange that someone with the name of Tramontano, a name common to this area, worked in Chicago, with someone like Madeline and the two of you ended up out here. Tell me about Kyla Tramontano and how you came to be in Chicago."

She shrugged. "It's simple. I grew up there. It seemed logical to go to school there, then to work."

"But, your name is so . . . well, it could easily fit

out here in the Southwest. And, so could you, with your looks."

"Very perceptive aren't you?" she judged with a rueful smile. "Actually, Griff, I was born in New Mexico. In Albuquerque."

"And your parents were . . ." he encouraged.

"My mother was Anglo. For a brief time, she was married to a Navajo man."

"Ah," Griff breathed, softly caressing her velvet cheek with his thumb. "That accounts for your dark hair and eyes. And that wonderfully sexy, fawn-colored skin. But it doesn't explain why you grew up in Chicago."

"My parents were divorced soon after I was born, and my mother took me back to her home, which was Chicago. I never knew my father. Never knew the Southwest at all until last fall."

"You never knew your father?" Griff groaned inside at the unforgivable tragedy. "Your father never knew *you?*" It sounded deplorable to him, an outrage that a person wouldn't experience his or her father. And it was lamentable that this man had never known his lovely, talented daughter. "How could he allow such a travesty?"

"My father had no alternative. Mother was an assertive woman, which is where I learned some of my behavior, I'm sure. When she decided to leave him, she left no traces as to her whereabouts. She even changed our last name. I've taken Tramontano only since I moved to Arizona. She was very bitter, and wanted no part of him or his life-style for herself or for me. My father came from a different world, and I suppose he found it too difficult to even try to find me. He was from some distant town on the Navajo Reservation, near a large canyon."

"Probably Chinle. It's at the entrance to Canyon de Chelly. Have you ever been there?" he queried, taking a drink.

Kyla shook her head negatively. "Canyon de Chelly sounds familiar. I've never been to that part of the country. What is it like? Beautiful?"

"Depends on your definition of beauty. It's stark. And isolated. Would you like to go sometime?" Griff's voice was low and serious.

"Oh, yes. I'm very curious about the area. And my father. I'll go, someday." Her face lit with the glow of the promise.

"Would you like for me to take you to Chinle, Kyla? I have business in that part of the state later this summer. I'll be glad to take you with me."

"Would you, Griff? I . . . I'd love to go!"

He nodded. "I would consider it a pleasure. Everyone should know their father. And every father should know his daughter, Kyla. I think yours will be very proud of you, and what you're doing with your native American designs. He should know that his daughter is founder of Desert Spirits. Someday they'll be renowned."

Kyla's dark eyes shimmered with pent-up emotion as she considered the prospects of meeting her father. "Do you really think so, Griff?"

"I know so. I can feel it. You have what it takes to make it. Skill, intelligence, driving ambition. Do you know where your father works or anything about him?"

She shook her head. He shrugged. "I'd like to help

you find your father, Kyla. I feel very strongly that you should know him. And that he should know you. Now is your chance."

Their eyes exchanged more feeling and emotion than words ever could. Hers glistened with a deeply grateful, admiring response. His walnut eyes caressed her, made love to her as they contemplated the previous personal exchange and anticipated the pending trip. Later, he would wonder why he had ever made such an offer. His caring for her was far too deep, and it scared the hell out of him.

In contrast, Kyla would consider Griff the most generous, casual man she had ever known. However, he was still secretive and held a part of himself back from her. What she saw and admired was his quiet strength. But what was he hiding from her? And why?

Kyla's glance traveled to The Stable's doorway. Wade and Madeline stood near the old stalls that actually housed horses over fifty years ago. "It's Madeline and Wade. Here we are!" she called.

The four of them chatted over drinks before lunch, with Kyla cheerfully paying, and no one objecting. Apparently Wade was accustomed to her assertive, female manners. It was taking some doing, but Griff was learning. Learning about this unique, beautiful woman who first intrigued him with her vulnerability. Now she intrigued him with her strength and the unusual combination of those two dissimilar qualities.

The luncheon was pleasant and the style show enjoyable, at least for the women. The models swayed their willowy bodies through picturesque archways and beside elaborate wrought-iron railings, enhancing the chic, Southwestern styles against the luscious backdrop of Spanish architecture. Afterward, Madeline and Wade returned to Tubac and her shop. Kyla and Griff headed for the old Tumacacori Mission, three miles away.

"What did you think of the style show?" Griff shoved his weight against the heavy grate of a door that led inside the historic mission.

"Oh, the styles were typical Southwestern, a mixture of cultures that will blend adequately with contemporary styles. But . . . ." Kyla strolled into the semitropical courtyard and sat beneath an unusually large apricot tree. "They can't compare with ours!" Her almost-black eyes glistened with pride.

Griff propped a foot on the concrete bench where she sat, his elbow braced on his knee. "How's that?"

"Ours are not a mixture. They are genuine Southwest Indian fashions, authenticated by a native American designer! Two, in fact!" She glowed with pride, and Griff thought how marvelous she looked, smiling in this lush setting of trees and fountains. She could easily be the model for her own designs.

He nodded. "Two? You and . . ."

"Actually, Griff, I'm . . . I'm a newcomer to all this! My training is definitely contemporary. Anyway, I'm a half-breed! I'm just now learning about my heritage." She laughed at her own description. "I'm talking about a genuine, full-blooded Navajo lady who works for me and is helping with the designs!" Her excitement was hard to contain, and Griff sensed the importance Kyla placed on these creations of hers.

"What? You mean you have an Indian woman who works for you?"

"Yes. Her name is Ed Nah Trailing Flower, and she

lived on the Navajo Reservation all her life before moving to Tucson. She knows about native American crafts. All of them, including costume designs!"

"Kyla, that's wonderful."

A rather smug grin graced her face. "It's better than anyone ever expected! Madeline knew her and advised me to hire Ed Nah because of her ability and experience with intricate beadwork and appliqués, which are designs in a different material sewn on a garment. But she knows so much more than that. She has worn versions of these clothes we're making, and has seen them on her mother and grandmothers and aunts! But what makes the ones we're doing so special is the handwork. Ah, the beadwork, and all sewn by hand! It makes these clothes we saw today look pale in comparison! Oh, Griff, I'm so pleased with what we're doing! It's exciting!"

"And you should be proud, Kyla. I think it means more to you than just another business."

She crooked her head and looked up at him. "It's a strange feeling. I feel . . . this sounds crazy." She stopped, embarrassed to continue.

"Go on," he encouraged.

She stood and pinched a willow leaf, wandering around the garden nervously. "I felt an instant affinity for this whole area, and now, for the Desert Spirits designs. I was one of those people who loved the desert the minute I stepped off the plane. The beauty of the mountains and valleys around Tucson appealed to me. But when I saw Tubac, I fell in love with it immediately! It's like . . . like I was meant to be here . . . doing what I'm doing with the Indian clothes." Her voice dwindled and she tossed the crumpled leaf into a gently rippling fountain.

"Kyla . . ."

She took a breath. "I know, Griff. You probably think I'm crazy. And maybe I am."

His voice was low and persuasive. "No, Kyla. I don't think you're crazy at all. I think you're responding to your heart."

She laughed nervously. "It's like a primitive urge. Something hidden deep inside me all these years. Oh, I know perfectly well where I'm from. I'm a city girl from Chicago, well-educated, knowledgeable about city ways. I'm not familiar with the West. Nor, with the Indians. But this is where I belong. My heart's roots are here. It was obvious immediately. Madeline worried that my decision to move out here was made too fast. But I knew this was right for me and still don't understand why."

Griff's hands rested on her shoulders, and he kissed the spot on her nape warmed by the sun. "I don't know what drew me to you that day. I'm still wondering why I bothered. But I do know that the attraction is still there. More than ever. My big worry is that you'll decide this wild country isn't for you, after all, and go back to Chicago."

She turned into his arms. "Oh no! I'll never go back, Griff! This is where I belong. In fact, I've been so excited thinking about the possibility of finding my father, it was hard to sit through the show today. I didn't realize how important it is to me."

He pulled her close. "Canyon de Chelly is our destination. It's deep in the Navajo Reservation, far from civilization. I'm taking you for a reason, you know. I need an Indian companion to blaze the trail in Indian country for this ole' redheaded cowboy."

Kyla gave him a smiling kiss and wrapped her arms around his middle. "Don't look to me for protection to keep you out of trouble. Remember my problem with the rules and regulations? My looks are deceiving. You saw what a mess I made of the last two Indian dances we attended. Actually, I need you to keep me out of trouble, Cowboy."

"It's a deal . . ." he murmured as his lips found hers again, sealing them with his strength and promise. A shuffling sound accompanied muffled voices from the mission's esplanade and broke up their embrace.

They walked arm-in-arm past other park visitors out to the ancient crumbling walls of the original two-hundred-year-old Tumacacori Mission.

"I can just see my models in front of this beautiful, old building, Griff. The earth colors will contrast with my creations and set off the designs and brilliant hues. It will give an authentic, Southwest flavor to everything we have. From a photographer's point of view, what do you think?" She stopped and framed the setting with squared hands.

"From a non-photographer's point of view, I think it would look great."

She took his arm and pulled him into the dank, cool building. "What do you mean non-photographer? You're the pro who agreed to do my layout."

"Only because you insisted. And I wanted another excuse to be with you."

She propped her hands on her hips. "Griff, what are you talking about? Almost every time I've seen you,

you've had a camera in your hands! And the other photos you did for me were great."

He placed his hand in the small of her back. "Come on, Kyla. Let's get out of here. This place gives me the willies."

They stepped outside into the sunshine again, and Kyla persisted. "Don't you like this setting for the portfolio snapshots?" She seemed disappointed.

"Oh, there are some very good outside shots here. I just think it's too dark and morbid inside. Over here, for instance, by this pomegranate tree, would make a good background, especially in the fall when the fruit is ripe and orange."

"See, you do have a photographer's eye!" she pronounced with satisfaction as they strolled beneath huge mesquite and poplar trees.

"I have a man's eye for a woman's beauty. And you are all I see, Kyla." Griff pulled her into his arms again and kissed her, long and hard. They ignored the tourists this time, lost in the fierce flame of desire.

A breeze whipped through the cottonwood and mesquite trees, rustling leaves above the couple locked together in a long-denied embrace. It was meant to be. They were sure of it. Together at last.

CHAPTER SIX

"Hey, Cowboy! You're going to get burned!" Kyla dipped a handful of crisp, cool water and dumped it generously on Griff's sun-warmed back. "Hmmm, you're a little steamed already!"

"Ahhggggg!" Griff bolted upright with a roar and lunged for her. "What are you trying to do, you damned little she-cat? Make me have a heart attack?"

With a delighted laugh she dove out of his reach, then bobbled tantalizingly. "Just didn't want you to go to sleep in the sun. It could be disastrous for your baby-tender skin! We wouldn't want you to burn your back."

"Sleep? How the hell can I sleep with you around? It would take a cold, insensitive zombie to be able to block you out of his mind long enough to sleep!"

"And obviously you're none of those," she mused delightedly.

"If it's a warm-blooded reaction you want, come

here. I'll show you what reactions you provoke when you're near me!"

Kyla tread water, her bikini-clad breasts bobbing in and out of the blue, shimmering liquid. "I'm not looking for reactions, Griff. I only want your company. There's nothing duller for a guest than her host falling asleep!"

"Ah, so it's attention you're craving. Actually, sleep is only one of my problems. I can never get enough when you're around. I had planned to talk to you about that, and there's no time like the present. Come here. You can solve my other problem right now." He leaned over the edge of the pool and extended a long arm toward her.

Kyla marveled at his masculine form, from his outstretched arm to his well-muscled chest, narrow waist, and tapered legs. Sun-bleached auburn hair covered his body, forming a thick mat across his chest and erotically encircling the large, deep-magenta aureoles. The hairline then narrowed to a trail that led down the center of his body below his navel. Her eyes traveled that sensuous streak to the darker pubic hair that curled around the edges of his black bikini. The area seemed to swell before her eyes, the tiny bikini barely covering what it was intended to hide from view.

"We don't really need these swimsuits, you know," he had advised earlier.

But she squeezed into hers saying, "Just in case your neighbors are watching."

"The pool is completely private; no one can see over the wall. But if they happen to sneak a peek, let's give them the complete, bare-assed show! They'll get their money's worth, at least!"

Kyla smiled, wondering if they were getting their money's worth now. Suddenly, she didn't care who was watching. "God, you're sexy, Cowboy! When you take your boots off, you're hard to resist." She reached for his hand and ran her own up the muscled contours of his arm.

"Come here . . ." he ordered gruffly.

In one easy movement he swept her out of the pool and onto that expanse of curly hair on his ample body. She drenched him with sweet, cool water as she pressed to his entire hot length. Sparkling liquid dripped from her breasts to his mouth as he bent to kiss each one, then sipped the rare nectar from her cleavage and the arched column of her neck. Their lips met to imbibe the eager intoxication each offered. Their kiss was a silent toast, sealing them together in steaming passion as they lay entwined, arms clinging to bare backs, smooth legs tangling with hairy ones.

"Ah, you're nice and cool," he murmured into her hair, kissing here everywhere.

"Griff," she finally muffled. "It's hot out here. Let's get back in the water."

"You don't want to spoil everything, do you," he grumbled, pressing his burgeoning groin against her.

"No," she admitted appreciatively and reached to cup his expanding masculinity.

"Ah, when you touch me, Kyla—" He moaned, then nibbled a damp furrow from her earlobes down the golden column of her neck to the still-moist valley between her breasts. Adept, masculine fingers untied the string behind her back that attached her bikini top, and it slipped below the pale ecru mounds. Her taut, burgundy nipples seemed to beg for attention and he obliged, teasing each between his tongue and upper teeth. Ever so gently, he tugged them to firm perfection.

"Griff, you don't want to give your neighbors the complete show, do you?" she objected weakly, not really wanting him to stop.

Resolutely, he pacified her by pressing her pliant breasts to his brawny chest. "I just want to feel you against me. See, I can hide you from anyone's curious view like this. Anyway, nobody's home this time of day."

"We act as though we have nothing to do but play," she scoffed, running her hand down the length of his muscular back.

"We deserve a day off, Kyla. Both of us have been putting in many long hours lately. Why, I've been working more for Desert Spirits than for my own company!"

Kyla's hand slipped sensuously beneath his bikini to grasp one tight male buttock. "Yes, and I appreciate it, Griff. But, Mavis is so competent, I feel sure she can handle things at the office."

"She's very efficient and trustworthy," he defended gruffly.

"I'm sure she is. Just so long as she keeps that efficiency at the office and out of my business with you," Kyla grumbled.

"Don't be too rough on Mavis. She's working very hard for Desert Spirits, too."

"Oh?" Kyla stiffened defensively.

"I probably shouldn't tell you this but—" He halted, knowing he had piqued Kyla's curiosity.

"But—what?"

"Oh, I'd better wait until we know for sure . . ."

"What is it? Tell me!" She wrapped her fingers threateningly around his neck.

"Oh, it's nothing much, really."

"What is nothing much?"

"Would you believe," Griff paused maddeningly. "Mavis is working on Goldwater's for your first show?"

"Goldwater's?" Kyla shrieked and wriggled excitedly. "Goldwater's exclusive department store? Oh, Griff!"

"Now, now, take it easy. I knew this would be a mistake. It's still in the planning stages. Don't move, Kyla. You don't want the neighbors to see all this glorious flesh, do you?" He crushed one errant breast with his palm.

"You claimed the pool was secluded and hidden from your neighbors' view. Plus, you said that no one else is home now! Just imagine, Griff," she demanded enthusiastically, "Desert Spirits at Goldwater's!"

"Yes, yes, it'll be wonderful. Ah, this is better, anyway." His large hands caressed and cupped each breast, lifting them to fullness against her ribs. When his tongue lashed out to gauge each pert nipple, she preened toward him, forgetting Goldwater's and Desert Spirits and thinking only of that tongue and the blazing fire it ignited in her body. He dipped to singe her navel with his devil tongue, then lower to her abdomen and thighs.

"We'd better go inside, Griff," she murmured. "It's wonderful here at night, but I feel very exposed in the daylight. I have no desire to be an exhibitionist."

"Only for me." He raised his head and smiled with

masculine approval at the swollen response her tawny breasts made at his touch.

"Only for you, Griff . . ." she said raggedly, finding it difficult to breathe as his tongue tormented her senses and made fiery trails on her inner thighs.

"Maybe you're right," he agreed, shifting to strain his achingly full manhood against her. "We'd better go before I burst the seams of this flimsy rag I'm wearing." He swept her into his arms and the bikini top dropped, unnoticed, into the shimmering, blue pool.

Their brown eyes met, filled with promises of what the next few moments of lovemaking would bring.

As he carried her inside the house, Griff was all too aware of the intensity of their relationship. He spent every waking moment thinking of her, dreaming of her silky, bare skin against his. Perhaps they were moving too fast. Loving too soon. Ah, but he would think about that later. When his mind was clear. When he didn't want her so badly.

He laid her on the bed and slid her bikini bottoms down long, trembling, tanned legs. Then his thumbs hooked the sides of his own tiny bikini and flipped it off quickly. His extended manhood sprang forth conspicuously, unhampered, as his eyes drank in her feminine beauty. Griff stood for prolonged, glorious moments gazing hungrily at her exquisite, golden body waiting for him.

Kyla's somber, native-brown eyes beckoned to him. Her jet-black hair, rippling with faint waves from her Anglo ancestors, the rise and fall of those burgundy-tipped, ecru breasts, the slender waist dotted with an inviting navel crevasse, the long, tanned legs joined at the dark-shaded juncture, were all his for the touching. For the taking. Intriguing, intimate thoughts drove him crazy with desire, and every masculine cell in Griff ached for her. He yearned to take her in his arms and make her his own as only a man can.

Kyla's legs slid sensuously apart. "Come on, Griff," she begged softly. "Don't make me wait any longer."

When Griff could restrain his passion no longer, he lowered himself to her. Settling himself between her legs, he moaned unthinkingly, "Kyla, my love . . ."

Even in that passionate moment, Griff's mind fought those feelings. *Oh my God, NO! I won't let myself love Kyla! I will help her, give whatever I can, but not my love! Ever!*

However, his body betrayed his resisting mind. Plunging deeply, feverishly, into her softness, Griff tried to forget that his love for Kyla was growing. Again and again he thrust vigorously, until they both crested in explosions of undeniable, heedless ecstasy. Afterward, he wrapped her in his arms tenderly. "Kyla, don't leave me. Love me . . . forever."

The photography session for the designer portfolio started early. Kyla rented a motor home to serve as a portable dressing room for the two dark-haired Indian models she had hired. It was an easy way to transport all her garments as well as the models to the various locations they needed.

Griff brought his assistant, Pasqual, and an impressive array of photography equipment that practically filled the Volvo wagon. They met in the vague dawn light to avoid the intense midday light and heat. The small crew murmured greetings, shared coffee from thermoses, and moved sleepily. Griff was the only one who alertly attacked the job at hand.

Kyla dressed the models, draping them with stunning turquoise and silver jewelry borrowed from Madeline and Ed Nah, then turned them over to Griff and Pasqual. For someone who could barely operate an automatic Minolta, she was impressed with the meters, zoom lenses, filters, reflectors, lights, and tripods Griff used in his work. Using a macro lens, he moved in close for beadwork detail. An ultrawide angle captured the full length of the models against gray-toned, weathered wooden doors and staid, adobe brick walls. Some of the shots were upbeat and energetic. Others captured a somber mood juxtapositioning adobe mission ruins with rich, brilliant Southwestern colors.

Watching from a distance, Kyla was definitely pleased with Griff's eye for lines, shapes, patterns, scale, and detail. He seemed to know, instinctively, how to portray each creation. He knew how she felt about these designs—possessive, excited, justifiably proud. Each garment was a part of her. She couldn't forget how much time she had spent explaining all this to him, and how patiently he had listened. He really did understand. Were she and Griff becoming of one mind?

It was thrilling to observe him at work. He became absorbed, almost mesmerized in it. He was oblivious of her and others around him. It was just Griff and his cameras and the models. By noon, with virtually no breaks except for traveling between Tubac and the Tumacacori Mission, they were finished. Kyla bought everyone lunch at The Stables before they parted.

"Tonight's on me," Griff promised, leaning close to

Kyla's ear. "We'll have our own private little celebration. Just the two of us. I'm pleased with the way things went today, and I hope you'll be satisfied, Kyla."

Kyla smiled appreciatively. "I know I will be, Griff. I'm completely satisfied that you know what you're doing behind a camera."

He quirked a crooked smile and drawled, "Why, that's the nicest compliment I've heard all day."

Her soft hand slid over his arm. "Well, Cowboy, I was very impressed with your skills. I hope you noticed how I managed to stay out of your way and refrain from kibitzing."

"Noticed? Why, I missed your guidance. I kept expecting you to help me read my light meter or, at the very least, change a model's elbow positioning."

"Not a chance! I wouldn't interrupt the artist at work! Actually, Griff, in my amateur opinion, some of the shots will be spectacular!" She pressed his arm. "I'm so excited about them, I can hardly wait to see the results!"

"Be patient, little lady. I hope they'll be worth waiting for. Give me a day to process them. Perhaps you'd like to accompany me to the darkroom, and we'll see what develops," he teased, kissing her temple.

"Ohhh . . . bad joke," she grimaced. "I'll leave the developing to the photographer, thank you. Didn't I hear an earlier invitation to dinner? Something about a celebration?"

"Hmmm. I want to take you some place beautiful. After the busy week we've had, I can't think of a better way to end it than dinner under the stars. You and me and the desert mountains!"

"Sounds wonderful. Where did you have in mind?"

"Some place we've never been before," he hinted obscurely and shoved his chair back. "We'll watch the Sonoran sunset over Nogales. I'll see you tonight about seven. This time, it's my treat. Don't you dare bring a dime." Griff growled in her ear, then kissed it sensuously.

"Not even a dime to phone home?"

"It's a quarter these days, little lady. I guarantee you'll be perfectly safe with me, but I can't promise you'll make it home afterward. I prefer a midnight swim, myself." His finger caressed her cheek quickly, then Griff was gone.

The lingering tingle of the kiss, his tender touches, plus the promise of an evening with Griff kept Kyla's anticipation high all the long, hot afternoon. When he arrived at seven, they drove straight south, toward Mexico.

Before reaching the border town of Nogales, he pulled the Jaguar to the hilltop location of the lovely Rio Rico Inn. On the balcony patio, a gentle night breeze lifted Kyla's dark hair as if cherishing its beauty, enhancing the elegant lines of her slender neck and shapely shoulders. Griff raised his glass to hers and the clink of crystal against crystal sealed their silent pledge. *To love.* But neither admitted it.

"*Salud.* To the fulfillment of your dreams, Kyla."

She smiled happily and the evening breeze sent a visible shiver through her. "To the success of Desert Spirits."

Of course, Kyla wanted success for her business. It was extremely important to her. But her heart's desire was another thing altogether. She felt a growing attachment to this auburn-haired cowboy named Griff Chansler. She couldn't dismiss the feelings she had for this man who thrilled her, pleased her with his expert devotion to her work, and satisfied her womanhood like no other man ever had.

"There is no doubt in my mind, Kyla. You've worked too hard, now. And your work is too fine. Success for Desert Spirits is inevitable. In fact, I have a message for you from Mavis. I know you'll be pleased."

"From Mavis?" she puzzled.

"Goldwater's contacted her today. They want to feature your designs in a special event they sponsor each year honoring the Southwestern Indian artists! Congratulations, Kyla! The world is about to see Desert Spirits!"

"Goldwater's? Oh, Griff—our first show! I can hardly believe it! I'm . . . I'm overwhelmed! And excited!" She squeezed his hand. "Thank you, Griff! This is the beginning of my dream!"

"Just the beginning, Kyla. Just the beginning."

She smiled happily. "First, Tucson—next, the world! Madeline will be thrilled. I think I'll go call her. Will you excuse me for a moment?"

"Do you need to borrow a quarter?"

"No thanks. I brought my own!" She whipped away from the table, then reappeared instantly. "What a miserable businesswoman I am, Griff! When is the show? Madeline will be sure to ask."

"I thought you'd reconsidered my offer of a quarter!" He smiled up at her. "It's in about two weeks. They want to meet you and see some of your samples. Is there something called a trunk show?"

"Yes. A trunk show."

"Mavis will call you tomorrow with the details. Do you have a trunk?"

She smiled and touched his arm affectionately. "No. But we'll certainly get one in a hurry! Be back in a minute."

Kyla returned flushed and smiling. "Madeline is very happy. And she thinks you're great!"

He shook his head slowly. "I keep telling you, this is Mavis' doing. What do I know about Goldwater's and trunk shows?"

"Then, Mavis is great!" Kyla sipped her drink with relish.

Griff raised his eyebrows. "I never thought I'd see the day you lauded Mavis!"

"Tonight, she's beautiful! So are you! And so is this place!" Her slender hand gestured to the green Rio Rico community and bare Mexican mountains.

His eyes followed hers to the distant horizon where the setting sun painted streaks of yellow and orange to offset the purple hills that hid the border town of Nogales. Beyond the shadowed hills were the larger mountains of Mexico. Serenity settled over the world as they sipped frozen margaritas.

As she settled down from the exciting news, Kyla reflected, "You know, there is something peaceful about the horizontal lines out here in the West. The stretches of space are definitely soothing to the spirit. It's dramatic and brilliant, and subdued, all at once. I think that's why people like me fall in love with this otherwise barren land."

His hand covered hers. "And people like me, who could never leave this strange country, are glad you came here and fell in love with it. Actually, when I look out, I don't see it as barren at all. It's covered with desert growth. Giant saguaros, growing only in this part of the world, all types of cacti, hardy mesquite and scrub oak, wild flowers . . ."

Kyla brought his hand to her lips, and kissed the palm. "You're right, Griff. It is unusual here. There is so much I have to learn about this country. And you."

His finger outlined her lips, following the natural lines, imprinting their shape in his mind. "I'll be your teacher. We'll start tonight."

"I can't think of a better teacher. Are you an expert on desert life?"

"No," he quipped dryly. "I was thinking of a different sort of instruction, little lady."

"Can't you ever be serious?" she complained, but couldn't help loving his bantering. *Loving him.*

"I'm very serious! A serious student of the desert. Now, take this margarita, for instance." He lifted his frosty goblet for display. "Did you know this flowered-up, frozen margarita is an American invention, supposedly first concocted in Los Angeles?"

"No," she responded, just as he knew she would.

"Well, understandably, the Mexicans were horrified at this tequila froth. You see, they drink it straight *con mucho gusto.*"

"Straight?" Kyla gasped, unbelievingly. "Doesn't it pack a wallop?"

"*Sí,* Señorita. They chug a shot glass of tequila, and follow it with a chaser of lime juice and salt. Or is it the other way around? Oh well, after a couple of them, nobody gives a damn which comes first!"

"Now, what would I do without this valuable bit of information, Señor Chansler?" she teased.

"Just thought it might broaden your knowledge. You never know when acquired trivia will come in handy. Why, just look at all I'm learning from you, Kyla. How not to behave at Indian ceremonials, for instance!"

"Please," she begged. "Don't remind me!"

"Actually I'm learning a hell of a lot about Indians from you. I thought the art of beadwork was practically extinct, but here it is alive in your designs. And I never knew a thing about basic Indian styles and how they differ from tribe to tribe and region to region. Now I know what a *manta* is, and that it's my favorite type of dress. Shoulders are sexy."

"Only one shoulder is revealed in a *manta*." She smiled. "Traditionally, it's the left."

"One's enough! See how much I'm learning?"

"It should be no surprise that you're fond of shoulders," she groaned.

"Speaking of surprises, when we go to Chinle, we'll be camping in Canyon de Chelly. I need to get some special shots, early morning, late evening, that sort of thing. I hope you don't mind roughing it a little."

"I'm adaptable," she proclaimed, while wondering if, indeed, she was that flexible. "So it's a photographic session?"

He shrugged. "Hmmm. Something like that. However, I'll try to keep it to a minimum to prevent you from becoming too bored."

"I can always take a good book."

"Damn, woman! I hope we don't have time for reading! I plan to keep you busy!"

"Busy? On a camping trip? I thought it would be a relaxing, get-away type of weekend."

"Oh, sure. It will be. But," he warned, "there's stoking the fire, making sure our sleeping bag is warm, enjoying the serenity . . ."

"What about just enjoying?" she murmured with a smile.

"Hmmm. That, too. I think I want to take you away now. For enjoying." He smiled devilishly.

"Not yet. I haven't even finished my cocktail. And you promised dinner, Griff."

He shook his head. "Always thinking of your stomach."

"Well, this margarita is very good. It'd be a shame to waste it."

"Would you like another?" Griff finished off his drink and called the waiter to order another round.

"No, thank you. I'll just nurse this one along. These things are pretty strong for someone who isn't accustomed to the wallop they pack," she laughed. "I'll be in trouble if I finish a second margarita before eating dinner. I'm an old-fashioned girl who can't hold liquor very well, especially on an empty stomach. Can't we order now?"

"Ahhh," he said teasingly. "All I need is to ply you with liquor!"

She touched his chin, letting her fingers trail along his jawline. "Unfortunately, I don't need liquor. You entice me enough."

"Ah, fortunately for me, little lady!" he amended. "And all this time I thought it was my pool at midnight! Can we forgo dinner? I think I want you right now!"

"I'm hungry!" she pouted. "You promised."

"I promised a beautiful sunset, and I delivered."

"Griff—" She cast him a threatening eye.

"I'll order," he acquiesced reluctantly. "But if I end up with indigestion, you may take the blame for causing me undue stress!"

She pointed accusingly at the frosty drinks before them. "Blame the devil tequila!"

"You're beautiful . . ."

"You're intoxicated!"

"Only by you, little lady." Their repartee was interrupted by the waiter, who patiently took their order. His presence prevented Griff from saying what was on his mind, that he was intoxicated with love for Kyla. Oh God, he didn't want to say that. He didn't want to admit it, even think it. He was just taken with her exotic beauty. And filled with undeniable lust for her. But that was all, he affirmed silently. No love involved!

When the meal was served, they spent the first ten minutes eating, not talking. "I told you I was starved!" Kyla said, taking a bite of crusty Mexican bread.

Griff nodded. "Our day started quite early."

"You did a wonderful job today, Griff. I don't know if I had a chance to thank you, but I do appreciate your skills." She leaned toward him seriously.

He smiled seductively. "You can thank me properly later, little lady."

"Button up, Cowboy," she snapped. "I'm being serious! I watched you work today, and I'm impressed."

" 'Tweren't nothin', ma'am," he drawled irritatingly.

"Dammit, Griff! There you go again! Can't you take

a compliment graciously? Is that the way with you macho cowboys?"

"Depends on what you're complimentin', ma'am."

"Well, I'm complimenting your professionalism today," she avowed. "No matter what you say, you're the best photographer I've ever seen work."

Suddenly, Griff was serious, too. His face veiled with a pensiveness as he muttered, "No, Kyla, I'm not the best. Not at all. My father was."

"Your father *was?*" Observing his change of expression, Kyla emphasized the last word, suspecting his response.

"Yeah. My father died last year. *He* was the best photographer in the West! The very best, better than Muench, Mann, Jacka, and all the rest! He just wasn't as well known."

Her hand reached for his. "Griff—"

"I guess I'm still bitter that he had to die just when we had so many good things going for us. We were working together at long last. He was vice-president of Chansler Marketing, Inc., in charge of photography. I . . . I depended on him, valued his advice. I still haven't found anyone to replace him."

"I'm sure you never will, Griff."

"No, never will. But, I—needed him. Still do. Like most strong-willed people, we had some rough years together. Even spent several years apart. Finally, we mended all those broken fences. I discovered what a fascinating guy my old man was. When he died, I lost my best friend."

"That's a beautiful thing to say about a parent. I'm sorry he's gone, Griff."

He shook his head, barely hearing her. "Then, he left that goddamn book unfinished . . ."

"What book?" Kyla leaned close to catch his low words.

"His book! That damn book I'm trying to complete. Northrup Press contacted me and asked if I would please fulfill his contract, reasoning that most of the work was done before his death. They persuaded me it was a book that should be finished, and like the sentimental dolt that I am, I agreed."

"Why is that so bad, Griff? Don't you want to do it?"

He shoved his empty plate away and ordered coffee for them. "I agree that it definitely should be done. Dad's idea was to make a photographic record of Indian life in the twentieth century. It will be a photojournalist's account of Southwestern Indians today, in their everyday lives, including how and when they mingle in the Anglo world and still preserve their own integrity and culture. Sort of a follow-up to Van Oorden's turn-of-the-century photographic exposé."

"That's why you've been going to all the Indian Dances," she deduced. "And why you said you were pulled into this against your will."

"Exactly. Even this trip to Canyon de Chelly is to take some photos for the book."

"You should be proud the publishing company thinks enough of your father's work to publish it posthumously."

Griff shook his head. "Actually, I'm torn, Kyla. The work done by my father is extraordinary, especially considering that he obviously wasn't a native Indian. His interest and empathy is obvious in his work. I just don't know if I—" He faltered and stared across the valley at the glittering Rio Rico lights.

"If you can measure up to his quality," finished Kyla.

"Yeah, I guess so," he sighed.

Her hand tightened on his arm. "Of course you can. From what I saw of your work today, Griff, I'm sure —"

"Don't try to indulge my ego, Kyla!" His tone was suddenly angry, and she responded just as smartly.

"Well, what the hell did you expect? You tell me about how terrific your father was, then how inadequate you feel. What did you want me to do except boost your ego!" She pushed her chair back and strode angrily to the railing at the edge of the patio.

After a moment, a steel-like, masculine arm encircled her shoulders and pulled her against a firm chest. "You're right, Kyla," he murmured. "I asked for it. I guess that tequila spurred a little self-pity that I didn't intend. What did I want? Your understanding, I suppose."

She turned and lifted her brown eyes to his. "I do understand, Griff. And I guess I was a little insensitive to your feelings just now."

"No, you were honest. That's something I need, too. Kyla . . . Kyla . . . I need you. Need your understanding and honesty." His fingertips lifted her chin and his lips tenderly kissed hers, expressing a million claims of love in that one touch. "I want you tonight," he muffled softly against her ear.

"Griff—" She struggled with the desire to embrace him right there in the restaurant. "I want you, too."

"Let's get the check and go."

She nodded and followed him back to their table. "Griff? Let's go back to my home."

His dark eyes were desirous pools of passion. "I thought I'd rent a room here at the inn, Kyla. It could be very private. They have a pool . . ."

"I feel . . ." She smiled and shook her head. "I want you to take me back home, please. I just have a feeling that I should go back. Maybe I want you in my own bed."

He shrugged. "Whatever you say, Kyla. Just don't send me away tonight."

"I want you with me," she promised, clinging to his hand as they walked past the huge outdoor entryway fireplace.

The eleven-mile ride back to Tubac was quiet, each reflecting on the day's work, the evening's revelations, the promised night together. Griff's strong arm pulled her close, and she maneuvered around the gears in order to be close to his chest. He gave her strength and security. Kyla rested her head on his shoulder and, if the ride had taken a little longer, she would have fallen asleep, snuggled against him.

Griff's low growl aroused her. "What the hell . . . ?"

The first portent of foul play was the broken window visible when they pulled into the driveway. Griff muscled his way into the house with Kyla right behind him. The upheaval flashed like a nightmare as they went from the kitchen to the front workroom.

Then she saw it. The closet doors hung open, although at a warped angle, as if someone had forced them. Except for a tattered piece of material caught in a hinge, the closet stood empty. *Empty!* They were gone! All the unique designs, her wonderful creations, her hours of work—stolen!

Kyla gasped, breathing hard and fast, fighting for the air that just couldn't keep pace with the demands of her heaving lungs. There wasn't enough oxygen! The walls were closing in around her! Suddenly, a high-pitched scream pierced the stillness of the night before everything went black for her.

CHAPTER SEVEN

The lights, blinding at first, filled Kyla's head and she could barely see Griff's hovering outline. She blinked, then moaned audibly, remembering. Was it really true? Or was this a horrible nightmare? Maybe too much tequila! She opened her eyes, this time focusing on Griff's concerned face and his rumbling voice.

"Hey, there, little lady. Are you awake? You okay?"

Her hand went instinctively to her head. "I suppose the next response is 'What happened?'" she groaned. "I'm embarrassed. I have never fainted in my life. I'm not the fainting type! I . . . I don't know what happened to me."

"I think you hyperventilated," Griff answered gently. "Here, smell this." He stuck something dreadful under her nose, and Kyla jerked away from the powerful aroma.

"My God! What the hell is that?" she rasped.

Madeline's pinched face peered over Griff's shoulder. "How is she? Sounds normal now with that smart-aleck tongue."

"I think she's on her way back." He conversed with Madeline as if Kyla weren't right there listening, trying to focus.

Kyla struggled up on her elbows. "What putrid concoction is in that bottle? It's enough to gag a—"

"This?" Griff looked curiously at the bottle in his hand. "Some kind of ammonia cleaning liquid. It was all Madeline could find. Bad, huh?"

"Horrid," Kyla grated between her teeth, swallowing hard.

He shrugged. "Well, it did the trick. You're looking somewhat more alive. Not quite so pale."

"That stuff will kill or cure! You two aren't very good at nursing! Now, what in hell is going on around here?" Kyla sat upright, then felt a wave of dizziness sweep over her. She leaned against the wall for support and tried to look past Griff's shoulder. "I may be sick."

"Now, Kyla, just take it easy. We've called the police, and they'll find out what happened. They'll get this all settled in no time. It's their job." His tone was soothing, his hands calmly resting on her shoulders.

She looked around the room. "Someone broke in here! And stole my collection!"

He nodded slowly. "Looks that way."

Kyla's eyes bore into him. "Griff, your protective, good-ole-cowboy manner is infuriating me. I am not a fragile 'little lady' that you need to protect! Now, would you please move so I can get up off the floor? I . . . I have to see . . ."

But he didn't move, just patted her arm sympathetically. "Now, Kyla. Why don't you wait a few more minutes?"

She pushed on his arm, irritated further by his stalling. "No! I want up! Would you please stop treating me like a child? I can handle this."

He eased back, resting on his haunches, and looked her in the eyes. "Now, how would I know what you can handle? The first thing you did in a crisis was to faint! I don't want to take a chance on that happening again."

"Oh, hell!" she scoffed. "That won't happen again. I have never fainted in my life. I hyperventilated after too much of your damned tequila tonight. Now, MOVE!" She struggled to her feet, holding onto Griff's arm for initial support.

Kyla stumbled into the workroom, where most of the damage had been done, and held onto the doorframe for support. With an audible moan, she stared at the empty closet. Kyla touched the inside wall and closed her eyes as if willing them to return. Even in the face of the bare, ugly facts, it was hard for her to believe that her entire collection of beaded designs had been seized.

She turned away before her emotions gave way to tears. Visibly shaken, she smothered a wailing sound and turned pain-racked eyes to Madeline, who stood helplessly wringing her hands.

"Who would do such a thing?" Kyla rasped.

Without a word, both women knew! They knew, but they didn't admit it. Didn't say it to each other. Didn't tell the police. There wasn't a shred of proof. Only intuition.

With the sound of a car out front, Griff announced,

"Here come the police. Don't touch a thing, Kyla." He went out to greet them.

Kyla quickly wiped a tear from the corner of one eye. This was no time for sentimentality. She had to be tough. She would be strong. But deep inside she wanted to wail and cling to Griff and awake in the morning to find everything back in place.

It was another hour before the police, with their fingerprint dusters and cameras and millions of questions, left.

Madeline wrapped her arms around her young friend, hugging Kyla close. "Oh God, Kyla! I'm so sorry!"

Kyla murmured sadly, "And we were supposed to have our first show in two weeks. Our first chance, shot to hell!"

"We can still do it, Kyla."

"It's impossible! I have nothing left!" Kyla gestured helplessly.

"Nothing is impossible!" Madeline said emphatically, as if to convince herself as well as Kyla. "Have you forgotten those two beaded shirts you were working on at my house? And this *manta* you're wearing. That's three."

"But you can't have a style show with only three outfits, Madeline."

"It's only a trunk show. We won't need many, just enough to impress people. We'll do it," Madeline stated simply. "It may be abbreviated, but we'll do it!"

"That's the fighting spirit!" Griff patted Madeline's back. "Never give up!"

"You bet!" Madeline smiled. "And Kyla is a fighter, too! We just have to decide to do it! Now, it's late and

I've got to hit the sack. We'll deal with this tomorrow." There was an air of mourning as they hugged again, for Madeline realized the amount of time and work that really went into the garments. They had lost their masterpieces.

"Yes, tomorrow . . ." Kyla nodded and half-smiled as her friend eased out the back door.

While Griff walked Madeline home, Kyla went directly to a drawer in the kitchen and pulled it open. She lifted her long, stainless steel knife and frantically dug under the plastic tray.

Her suspicions were confirmed. The original sketches—all of them—were gone from her hiding place! They, too, had been stolen.

"Damn! Damn! Damn!" Kyla wailed, and, in an act totally out of character for her usually placid temperament, she plunged the knife with all her strength into the old, rustic table. It wedged in an ominous, upright position in the wood.

"Easy now, little lady," Griff soothed cautiously as he stepped inside the door. He moved quickly to her side, his hands reaching for her quivering shoulders.

Kyla stared at the knife as if she couldn't imagine how it got there. Then, pained brown eyes met his. "He took everything . . . my sketches, too . . ."

"He? Kyla, do you know something I don't?"

She responded alarmingly fast. "No! I just used 'he' as a general term. It could have been a woman."

Griff shook his head and sighed heavily. "I don't need to tell you this is a damn poor hiding place. Kyla, this new information should go to the police."

"Can it wait until tomorrow?" she asked weakly. "I don't think I could face them again tonight. It's just been too much—" The words choked in her throat as she thought of rehashing everything with the police.

"All right, Kyla," he conceded. "It has been a rough night for you. I wonder why he, or they, didn't steal everything they could lay their hands on. The toaster, the TV, your radio are all here, and yet, they would be easier to fence than the clothes you designed. It just doesn't make sense."

"Maybe we surprised them when we drove up." She found herself searching for excuses for the theft, just to appease her own mind.

Griff shook his head. "It's as if they merely intended to sabotage your business."

"Yes," Kyla nodded, still in shock. "Sabotage . . ." It was beginning to make sense. Only *he* would stoop to such treachery; only someone with such a blinding ambition that he could be driven to most any length. The thoughts frightened her.

"Kyla," Griff asked sharply, "do you know anyone who would want to ruin this business of yours?"

"No—" she lied, not looking into his eyes.

"What about the women who work for you? Jealousy, perhaps?"

Her answer came instantaneously. "No! Oh, God, no! Not Carmen! Definitely not Ed Nah! They worked too hard! I'm sure of it! I have already explained all that to the police, Griff. Surely you believe me!"

"I know, I know. I'm just grasping at possibilities."

"We've already been through this, Griff," Kyla said, wearily brushing her hand over her forehead.

Tenderly, his large hands cradled her face, while his lips brushed her nose and lips soothingly. "Kyla, oh Kyla."

She looked deep into his sincere brown eyes. "All that time, all that work, all those originals, oh, Griff—" Finally, the tears came, hot and heavy and uncontrollable.

He drew her against his strong, secure chest, holding her close, giving the strength and sympathy she needed. She sobbed onto Griff's chest, allowing her feelings to pour forth with someone she had grown to trust and love.

Finally, she whispered, "Griff, don't leave me tonight . . ."

"I won't, Kyla. I won't leave. I'll stay as long as you want me." But, in his heart, even as he cradled her against him, he knew he wouldn't stay that long. He would stay only as long as he felt he could without getting too involved. Or was he already too involved? That thought haunted him as they slipped into her bed together.

Sometime in the night, the generous compassion between them turned to smoldering passion. Kyla cried heartbrokenly in Griff's arms, then dozed fitfully, cuddled on his warm shoulder. Her face rested against the auburn mat of hair that cushioned his solid chest. The sound of his heartbeat, pounding rhythmically in her ear, eventually broke into her consciousness. She stirred.

For a long moment, Kyla thought only of the extreme pleasure of being in Griff's secure arms. His warmth, his fragrance, his strength were all hers tonight. Then her eyelids fluttered open, and she remembered the horror that she would have to face in the morning.

"I keep seeing that empty closet—" she rasped.

Kyla lifted her face and met Griff's dark eyes gently watching her. He could see the pain, the vulnerability in her smoky brown orbs. Ah yes, she was a victim tonight. Defenseless. She needed him. And he took comfort in that knowledge as he pulled her close.

"Don't think of anything, Kyla. Nothing but us," he murmured in a low, sexy voice and kissed her cheeks. With velvet lips, he closed her eyes. "Things will be better tomorrow, but I can make you forget tonight . . ."

"Griff . . . oh, Griff, yes . . ." She arched her neck and he obliged with a moist trail of kisses to her earlobe, then down to her sensitive pulse points. "I'm glad you're here with me. I don't think I could face this alone."

"Kyla . . . let me make you forget everything. I'll love you tonight . . ."

"Griff, you're so good to me. First, the time and care you took making the portfolio photographs this morning. Then a lovely dinner. Now you're caught up in my personal problems. I wouldn't blame you if you left and didn't return."

"I can't do that, Kyla."

"But . . . why? You could have someone in your bed for a lot less trouble than me." She allowed her finger to trace his jawbone, then down his neck.

"I keep reminding myself of that," he observed dryly, with a faint smile crooking his angular face.

"Griff, I'm serious."

"Me, too. I want you, Kyla. No more questions. No meaningful answers. No commitments. Let's just enjoy each other."

"Your touch is heaven." She smiled. "I'm glad you stayed."

He cupped each exposed breast, lifting them to his mouth for tingling nibbles on the tips. Her response to him was instantaneous, the rounded mounds swelling with aching firmness. She thrust them upward as his tongue laved around the dark aureole, then tasted the taut burgundy nipples with obvious relish.

Kyla's eyes grew heavy-lidded with ecstasy as she watched his pink tongue reach again and again for the firm morsels, fondling them into tight knots of pleasure, sending sensations spiraling to the core of her senses.

"Oh, Griff . . ."

His thumbs and forefingers pulled gently. "You have beautiful breasts, Kyla. I love to touch them. To taste them. Your skin is so smooth, like silk. Do you know the first thing I noticed about you that day at the Indian ceremonials?"

"Obviously, my breasts," she chuckled. "You men are all alike."

"No, we are not all alike," he answered indignantly. "Surely you know that by now. You wore that backless sundress, and I thought you had the most beautiful back in the world!" His hands caressed her shoulders while he again kissed her ever-tautening breasts.

"Griff—"

"It's true. Then I saw your legs. Damn good legs!" His hands flowed down her body, stroking and massaging along the way to her long legs. His touch tantalized her inner thighs and she stretched one smooth leg over his rough one.

Her fingers roamed through the masculine hair on

his chest. "Do you know the first thing I noticed about you that day, Griff?"

"My chest," he mumbled, mocking her. "Or was it lower? You women are all alike."

"We are not!" she protested. "I noticed your boots. And I wondered what kind of man walked in those dusty cowboy boots." She extended her leg down the long length of his hairy one until her toes entwined with his.

He slid one arm under her hips, shifting her until she was almost lying atop him, her back against his chest. Both large hands reached her thighs, alternately massaging and stroking higher and higher. "And now that you know me? What kind of man have you decided I am?"

"Oh, you're somewhat macho and . . ."

His fingers continued their maddening explorations, finding the core of her femininity.

". . . and kind of gentle and . . ."

With feathery, zephyr-like motions, he enflamed her passion almost beyond duration. "Yes, go on," he prompted dispassionately.

"And—oh God—damned sexy!" She writhed against him as his hands roved from her swollen breasts down her sides to probe her most sensitive areas to low-moaning abstraction. "Griff, please—don't wait!"

"Turn over." His command was low and urgent.

With his help, she managed to roll over, pressing on the very hardest part of him. Sensations washed over Kyla that she had never felt before and with such intensity that she quivered with anticipation.

Griff smiled confidently up at her. "Now, little she-cat, let's see who's so damned macho. You are in the power position. The dominant one."

"Griff . . . help me . . ." She pushed on his chest, moving frantically to assuage her urges.

His large hands lifted her, joining them together in a wild clash of fervid passion like neither had ever experienced. The sensual feelings transcended personal feelings, binding them with a stronger bond of emotion than either cared to admit. There was a giving, a taking, a loving between them, never to be negated. Denied, perhaps, but not obliterated.

After the loving, the intensity of feelings, the heated explosions that rocked them both, Kyla slumped against Griff's pounding chest. She burrowed her arms beneath his shoulders and pressed herself tightly to him. "Hold me, Griff," she begged. "You're everything I want in a man. Everything I need. Don't leave me . . . ever."

Griff's hands spanned her back, clasping her to him. With silent aching, he listened to her poignant plea. Their hearts blended, pounding the excitement they had shared, finally slowing in contented satisfaction. As originally avowed, he shared a mutuality with Kyla, but Griff refused to heed his own heart. He held Kyla tenderly, lovingly stroking her back. Yet he could not say what he felt. Would not.

Griff wouldn't allow himself to truly express his feelings. For, if he had, at that moment he would have told Kyla he loved her.

During a time that should have been for growing love and tender affections between them, Kyla and Griff seemed to grow apart. Kyla was busy preparing for the show. Griff chose to work on his father's book or late at the office or anything that would keep him away from her.

Madeline and Kyla met with a Goldwater's representative and, in a moment of rash abandon, vowed they could be ready for a limited style show in two weeks. That promise threw them into first gear, and they worked day and night to replace their destroyed garments. Kyla was a whirling dervish of redesigning, reordering, purchasing, and making trips into Tucson. Somehow, there was no time for Griff. And he certainly didn't make himself available. Kyla knew, deep in her heart, his absence was purposeful.

As the date for the show drew closer, Kyla began a rudimentary course in learning the various styles of beading for their unique fashions. Ed Nah was a patient teacher, but Kyla proved to be an impatient student. She wanted instant results, and beading required infinite calm and diligence. She struggled with the difficult flat method, requiring millions of beads individually sewn in colorful lines that eventually formed a bold, traditional Indian design. She found it much more to her liking to design a contemporary garment and sprinkle the bodice with silver and turquoise beads. However, her pride and joy was a beautiful, floor-length *manta* of blue basket-weave silk.

Ed Nah drew on her knowledge of the traditional dress of the Hopi women, and Kyla added a contemporary touch to produce an unusual *manta* of exquisite beauty and striking drama. Long, elegant fringe angled from the one attached shoulder seam across the front bodice and down the entire length of both sides. The fringe was then beaded with turquoise, jet, and coral. One side was gracefully slit to the thigh for fluid movement and a sexy view of the model's leg. The two women shared a tremendous pride in their new product, a blending of ancient and modern, traditional and contemporary.

It was an exciting time of new creations and endeavors, which Kyla wanted to share with Griff. But he wasn't there for her. She couldn't help wondering if he ever would be again.

On the day of the show, Kyla tried to calm her nerves and get things organized backstage. She would wear the long *manta* and narrate the show. They hired three models to show the garments, and Madeline was in charge of helping them dress and keeping order to the apparent chaos.

Kyla brushed her thick, jet hair back and knotted it efficiently on her head. She looked even more exotic with the updrawn hair, for her dramatic cheekbones and the slight tilt to her dark eyes were emphasized. "Do you think he'll come, Madeline?"

"I don't know, honey. I wish you wouldn't bank on it."

"Mavis said Pasqual would be here to take pictures. Why won't Griff come? He knows how much this means to us! Our first show!"

Madeline smoothed the *manta* on its hanger and sighed. "I don't understand the man, Kyla. Looks to me like he's running from you."

Kyla attached large turquoise earrings with nervous fingers. "Maybe he's trying to tell me something."

"He said he was busy."

"No one could be busier than we've been these past two weeks!"

"He's been out of town, Kyla."

"Conveniently!" she grated and slipped her arms into the *manta*.

"Oh my God!" Madeline breathed in total admiration as she stood back and stared. "I wish he could see you now, Kyla. You're . . . you're gorgeous! And, I must admit, I've never seen you look more like your Indian ancestors!"

Kyla smiled impishly. "I am Indian! In part, anyway! And I'm going to scalp one big, red-headed cowboy! Now, help me attach this *manta* pin." Madeline held the material while Kyla applied the huge, fist-sized turquoise and silver pin to the shoulder that held the front and back panels together.

"Fabulous!" Madeline smiled into the full-length mirror that reflected Kyla's image.

"You know something, Madeline? Ed Nah should be here. She should be wearing some of these designs. I want her to be in the next show!"

"Next show? Why, we haven't even had our first one yet! And already you're talking about the next show!"

Kyla smiled reassuringly. "Of course, Madeline. There will be another show! This is only the beginning for us!" She repeated Griff's words, then turned to the other models. "Ready, girls? I think we'd better get started!"

She peered through the makeshift curtain at the growing crowd, gathering for the premier showing of the unique Indian fashions. Taking a deep breath, Kyla walked to the podium; Desert Spirits designs reached the public eye without the presence of one laid-back, redheaded cowboy.

It was nearly dusk when she approached the low, sand-colored building. She breezed past the *Changing Woman* painting in the lobby, but experienced a certain power that gave her mission even more determination.

"Thank you for letting me in, Mavis. I know it's nearly closing time. I just want to see Griff for a minute."

"How was the show?"

Kyla smiled warmly. "It was wonderful! My clothes were very well received! We sold several garments and have orders for others! Thank you, Mavis. It was an excellent idea!"

Mavis' face crinkled into a smile. "I'm glad. That's what we're here for, Kyla. To help get your business off the ground. Griff is in his office."

Kyla nodded and walked down the quiet hall. Almost everyone had gone, and Mavis was flipping off the lights. Soon they would be alone. Without knocking, she opened his office door and stood in the doorway, staring at him for a full minute. She caught her breath at the sight of him behind the desk, his auburn hair slightly disheveled, his sleeves rolled up, his mouth caught in surprise. Would she be able to carry this off? Could she tell him what she came to say? Her heart pounded a staccato beat inside her breast.

CHAPTER EIGHT

Where the hell have you been? That was what she wanted to ask him, wanted to scream at him. However, when Kyla saw Griff, she melted inside and couldn't muster that much acidity to rail at him. The sight of him did funny things to her insides, and suddenly all the pent-up venom slithered away, and she wanted to bury her face and run away. But running away from obstacles wasn't her style. Confronting them was!

"Where . . . where have you been?" Her voice sounded mild compared to the cacophony inside her head at the moment.

His large hands turned upward in a casual shrug. "Where have I been . . . when?"

She stepped inside the room. Never had Kyla felt such trepidation; never had she felt such strange tuggings at her heart. It was a frightening feeling of losing control. Her emotions. Her heart. Her soul were awakening to new heights of feeling, of expression. What was happening to her? Oh God—she wasn't herself!

"Griff—you missed our first show! How . . . how could you? Why?"

He stood then, a torn expression on his face. "I know. I was busy, Kyla. How did it go?"

"Do you really care?"

"Yes, of course. I would have gone, but—"

"I know. You didn't want to get involved." She shakily grasped the arms of a chair nearby and slumped into it.

"No! That's not it, Kyla. I . . . I've just been so damned busy working on my father's book! We're trying to wrap it up, decide what to include and what to eliminate. It's hard to do, especially when the man who accumulated all the material isn't around to help."

She looked at him and blinked. Suddenly, she saw another side of Griff. He was a man struggling with his past, making difficult decisions that would perpetuate the work and memory of his father. Her heart melted, and she realized how important this was to Griff. Her first style show wasn't his top priority. Maybe she wasn't, either.

"I . . . I'm sorry, Griff. I know you've been busy. Mavis told me."

"Tell me about the show." His voice warmed. "Did Pasqual get photos?"

"Yes," she nodded. "It was a good show. We were well received. Even made a few sales and took several orders."

He sat back down. "Then you're off and running.

This is just the beginning for you, Kyla. Desert Spirits' beginning."

"Thanks to Chansler Marketing." She smiled tightly.

"Realistically, I know you would have made it anyway. But I'd like to think we helped."

There was an uncomfortable pause, then Kyla took a deep breath. "Well, I . . . I've got to go." Her whole purpose for being here had gone haywire, and she felt that she would explode if she sat facing him another minute. She rose and started for the door.

Griff stood and followed her. It was clumsy and quiet for a moment. "Kyla? Are you still willing to go to Canyon de Chelly? I told you we're trying to wrap up this book, and I need some photos from that area. I thought I'd go this weekend."

"I don't think so, Griff." She shook her head stiffly.

"Kyla, I want you to go." His hand circled her wrist. "Please."

She gazed up into his sincere brown eyes. "From the way you've been acting lately, I thought just the opposite."

"I explained that. I've been busy. We both have!"

Too busy for each other? she wanted to say. But she knew the answer.

"Anyway, Kyla, we're going to find your father. That is more important than anything either of us is doing right now. We must find him." There was an urgency to his voice.

"You really believe that, Griff?"

"I certainly do! You have to go! We'll leave Sunday morning, early. Why don't you drive up to Tucson Saturday night? We'll have dinner and . . ."

"And a midnight swim?" She smiled wryly and shook her head. "I'll drive up early Sunday morning. What should I bring? I don't have much camping equipment. In fact, I don't have any!"

"Just bring yourself. I can supply everything we need."

"Make sure you have two sleeping bags," she said, and opened the office door.

"Kyla—"

But she continued down the hall and outside. Damn him, anyway! She couldn't even say no to this trip! But, in her heart, Kyla knew this trip was extremely important. She had to find her father. He was the key to knowing more about herself, about her heritage. Griff knew it, too. He knew she had to go!

True to her word, or was it stubbornness, Kyla drove to Tucson early Sunday morning. Griff was waiting and handed her a steaming mug of coffee. They exchanged a few words over coffee but neither felt sure of the other at this point. They had shared such intimacy, then broken apart. Griff had shown his reluctance to become involved with her, and Kyla had made it clear when she agreed to go with him this weekend that she had called a halt to their intimacy.

Kyla stood, hands wrapped around the warm mug, watching the lights of the city twinkle in the early morning humidity. The view from Griff's front yard was spectacular, morning or night, and always entranced her.

"Ready to go?" It was more a declaration than a question. Griff slammed the back door of the Volvo, which was loaded up to the windows.

She smiled at him, feeling a little bleary-eyed in the

hazy dawn but happy nonetheless to be with Griff again. "Yep. Ready!"

As she and Griff drove northward from Tucson, Kyla glanced over the piles of paraphernalia in the rear of their vehicle. "Looks like we have enough junk to last a month! Everything but the kitchen sink!"

"Well, we may decide to stay a month. And, I can assure you, you won't find a kitchen sink where we're going!"

She shook her head firmly. "I can't stay longer than the few days we planned, no matter how much I like Canyon de Chelly."

"Even if we find your father?"

"Even then," she avowed. "I have too much work to do, Griff. Have you forgotten that my business was practically destroyed? Why, I have—"

"I know, I know, Kyla," he interrupted. "You've been under a lot of pressure lately and working overtime on your designs. That's why this little weekend trip will be good for you. Good for both of us."

"You're right. It'll be good to get away for a little while," she admitted with a sigh, leaning back on the headrest. "I know this sounds crazy, but it's a relief to leave it all behind. Worrying about the burglary, dealing with the police and insurance companies, trying to rebuild our stock as fast as possible, plus the Goldwater's show have left me exhausted. I hope I can relax."

He glanced at her profile and smiled. "Where we're going, there is nothing to do but relax! This can be a long, lonely trip. I'm glad you decided to come. You're pretty good company. Anyway, with your Indian appearance, we'll breeze into Indian country. Redheaded cowboys attract attention. Dark-haired ladies with high cheekbones don't."

"Good company!" she squealed with irritation. "Is that why you brought me along? To keep you from getting bored? And from getting in trouble with the Indians?"

He laughed. "That, and other things. How are you at warming cold feet in a sleeping bag? Can you start a campfire?"

"I told you, separate sleeping bags!" Even as she protested loudly, Kyla knew she wouldn't be able to resist lying in Griff's arms tonight! "For your information, Mr. Chansler, I've never slept in a sleeping bag! Nor have I started a campfire. Or cooked over one, for that matter!"

"Oh-ho! Are you in for a rude awakening! I'm putting you in charge of meals!"

"You'd better watch your step, Griff Chansler. I may dump you in the middle of Indian country and let you fend for yourself!" She folded her arms determinedly and glared out the window at the strange landscape of cholla cacti and giant yuccas.

"Knowing your experiences with the Indians, I'd better hang around to keep you out of trouble, little lady!"

"True," she laughed. "I suppose I'd better stick close to my cowboy. You're pretty handy to have around."

"Handy to have around? Now, who's using whom?" Griff scoffed, feigning disgust.

"Sorry if you're offended, Cowboy. The truth hurts, I know," Kyla provoked with a teasing smile.

"The real reason I'm taking you, Kyla"—Griff's

voice was suddenly serious—"is so you can find your father." At least, he was trying to convince himself that the only reason he wanted Kyla with him was to set her relationship with her father right.

She glanced across the seat at Griff and noted his pensive expression. "It is, isn't it, Griff?"

"Yes. Aren't you anxious to meet him?"

She smiled. "I'm looking forward to it. But you're assuming he is still living in this little town on the Navajo Reservation. And that he wants to meet me."

"Oh, he will. And, if he isn't here, someone will know where he is. We'll find him."

"This is very important to you, isn't it, Griff?"

He nodded silently.

"Your relationship with your own father must have been very good. Tell me about him. What was William G. Chansler like?" she encouraged.

Griff chuckled low in his belly as he recalled his father. "My relationship with William G. wasn't all that wonderful until about eight years ago. Part of it was my fault. I was rash and cocky and thought I knew everything. After college and a stint in the Navy, I returned to Tucson and, as the old saying goes, my father suddenly gained great knowledge and insight after those years of my youth. I think we both probably changed a little. Maybe a lot. I listened to him for the first time in my life. And he stopped trying to impose his values on me. Then we became great friends, even business partners."

"Impose his values?" Kyla puzzled.

Griff nodded. "I've told you he was a great photographer. And he thought everyone should love photography as much as he did. Especially me. Of course, I didn't. Part of that was just natural rebellion. Dad was like an artist. Produced great stuff. But he didn't get the breaks or acclaim he deserved. Nor did he achieve all he wanted to with his talent. He saw me as filling that chasm. Although I learned a lot from him on photographic excursions with him as a kid, I never loved it like he did. I objected like hell when he wanted me to take over certain aspects of his business. I wanted my own. And it wasn't photography."

Kyla interjected, "But, your marketing business relies heavily on photography."

"After many years of separation and personal agony, we came to see that working together was the only way. After we formed the business, he dropped the protective father role and became my dependable partner. There were even times when he was my best friend. Like when my wife died."

Kyla's eyes lifted quickly. It was the first time Griff had mentioned having had a wife. "When was that?"

"Six years ago. She died after a car wreck."

There was an uncomfortable silence. "How long were you married?" She knew it didn't really matter, but groped for something to keep him talking about this other woman in his life.

"Three years."

"I'm sorry, Griff. What a terrible tragedy."

"Yes. It was."

"How did it happen? Would you tell me about her?"

His lips tightened. "I'd rather not talk about it."

She looked away. "All right. I just . . ."

"I know, Kyla. I probably shouldn't have mentioned it. But I thought you should know I had been married at one time in my life. That's all a part of my past, though, and I prefer to keep it that way."

"Sure, Griff. Whatever you—"

His hand slid over hers. "What about you?"

"Huh?"

"Have you ever been married?"

Suddenly, the questioning was reversed. She turned back to him. "No. But I lived with a man once. I thought I was in love."

"You weren't?"

She shook her head. "No. It turned out to be one of my biggest mistakes. It has been very hard to break away from that relationship."

"Do you still hear from him?"

Kyla's eyes rounded with alarm. She didn't want to open that horrible, secret door that would reveal Ian in all his deviousness. So, she lied. "No. I don't think he knows where I am."

"Is that purposeful?"

She nodded. "I don't want to see him again. Ever."

"What is he like? What kind of person?"

"Why do you want to know?"

He shrugged. "I just would like to know what kind of man you lived with. What kind of man attracted you."

"I guess that's why I wanted to know more about your former wife, Griff. I wondered what kind of woman you chose as a wife."

He nodded slowly, then began speaking. "Fair enough. Shari was blond and not very tall and . . . oh God, not like you at all, Kyla. She did public relations work for another company. That's how we met. When we married, she came to work for us. There was quite a bit of nepotism at Chansler Marketing, with Shari and my dad working there. Now, they're both gone . . ."

His hand still rested, tightly now, in Kyla's. The palm was unusually moist and she could tell that talking about his former wife was traumatic for Griff. So, she picked up on her contribution to the conversation. "Well, Ian is nothing like you, either, Griff. He's much more slender and has a dark, goatee beard. He definitely isn't a cowboy. He's a talented designer, which is how we met. We worked together at Market Design and thought we were in love—" She paused, knowing she was close to revealing things she didn't want exposed. "There. Is that enough? Are you satisfied?"

"I'm satisfied with you, Kyla. I think you appeal to me because you're not at all like Shari. You're . . . unique. You're yourself, and I like that."

She squeezed his hand. "You're very distinctive, too, Cowboy. A man of resolve who pleases me."

"I thought I was too macho!" he laughed.

"I thought I was too assertive!" she countered.

His hand slipped out of hers and around her shoulders. "Come here, woman. I want to feel you close to me!" He pulled her across the seat to snuggle next to him.

"Even at six in the morning?"

"Why not? I want you close all the time!"

She reached up to kiss his earlobe. "How's this?" she whispered with a giggle.

"I'll give you an hour and a half to stop that! And we may never make it to Chinle today!"

She smiled and relaxed against his chest, while her hand rested on his thigh. The barriers had been breached; sour words and differences forgotten. They were again in each other's arms, where they belonged. Or did they? Was it possible for her to find happiness with a cowboy? Kyla pressed his hand to her cheek and fervently hoped so.

If his claim to have her near all the time was true, why hadn't he called her and made the effort to bring them together? What did Griff want; what did he need? Could she provide it? He seemed to step away, just when they drew too close. She still had too many doubts about their relationship to feel sure of him. But her feelings for him were powerful, and she could only go on present instincts.

They rode quietly as the terrain changed from high desert to pine-covered mountains to bare sheer cliffs of vermilion. They were content with each other, with the present.

Griff looked at the raven-haired woman beside him. Had things gone too far with this cosmopolitan lady? He feared the control she seemed to have over his thoughts and desires.

Kyla felt that Griff was the most interesting and understanding man she'd ever met. However, she doubted her own good judgment. He was far too different—and difficult—a man for her suave tastes. He was, after all, a cowboy. She glanced boldly at him, reached up and caressed his roughened cheek with her artistic fingers. Touching him was such a delight. Her lips softly kissed that spot on his cheek.

"Hmmmm. What was that for?"

"Just for . . . being here," she answered simply. "With me. For bringing me up here."

Whatever was in Kyla's imagination about the small

town in Arizona where her father lived was not epitomized by Chinle. It was not "Small Town, U.S.A." It was a remote Indian settlement, and there was a tremendous difference. Knowing her fashionable mother, Kyla wondered what had attracted her to a man who knew this isolated place as home.

Then, inwardly, she had to laugh at herself. What attracted her now to someone like Griff Chansler? A cowboy, for God's sake! They were as different as could be, and yet . . . neither could doubt the sparks that ignited between them. In another era, perhaps they would have married, maybe produced a child, as did her parents. It was a sobering thought.

"Why don't we stop in the Trading Post?" His voice startled her.

"Huh? Yes. Sure." Kyla stared at the square store, straight out of the old West, probably built a hundred years ago. She gaped at the worn-smooth hitching post, realizing that horses were tied—hitched—there daily while their owners browsed inside this forerunner to the department store. Curiosity about the interior of the trading post gripped her, and Kyla scrambled after Griff's ambling gait. She felt like an actor in a Western movie as she made footprints in the dust and stepped inside the plank-floored building.

Griff bought them two Tabs, then chatted with the man behind the counter about the weather, directions to various points of interest, and the whereabouts of a man named Kyle Tramontano. Kyla browsed through gorgeous turquoise jewelry and luxurious Navajo rugs, alongside ordinary groceries and garden tools. At the mention of her father's name, she ambled back to stand beside Griff, trying to get a grip on her racing emotions.

"I don't know Kyle Tramontano," the darkly tanned man said. "But I'm sure my mother does. She has known everyone around here for over seventy years."

"Could we talk to her?" Griff asked.

"Sure." He motioned to a young man who sat in the corner chair, pitched back on two legs and resting against the wall.

"Pablo. Take these people to your grandmother. They want to talk to her about a man who used to live here."

Pablo put aside his whittling and sauntered outside while Griff and Kyla thanked the man at the Trading Post. They drove out in the cloud of dust billowed by Pablo's truck, barely able to read its euphemistic bumper sticker proclaiming "Pick 'Um Up."

"Those Indians," commented Griff, as he wheeled along in the dust. "They still have a sense of humor along with their pride."

"It's . . . it's unbelievable," mumbled Kyla, not referring so much to the bumper sticker or the Indian's sense of humor as to the desolate place where they now searched for her father. She wondered if her mother had ever been out here. Her parents had lived in Albuquerque for a brief time after her birth, and even that city was too remote for her urbanite mother. But *this* . . .

"My God!" Griff marveled when they stopped. Both of them stared at the rounded earthen hut before them.

"I didn't think people still lived in hogans, Griff."

"Oh, yes, Kyla. This is another world out here. Are you ready to find out about your father?" He gripped her hand and smiled a tight, mirthless smile. It was a gesture that reassured her. Griff might be completely different from her, but at the moment he was with her, mind and spirit. "Let's go in."

They entered the dark, musty building and sat on a low sofa before a very old, wrinkled Indian woman. She squinted through wire-rimmed glasses at the two newcomers. Pablo prefaced their meeting with a few singsong sounds, words of another language, then sat on a low stool nearby. "This is my Grandmother Dezbah."

The grandmother lifted her head proudly to them. "Welcome to my home. You come from far away?"

"Yes, we traveled all the way from Tucson. I am Griff Chansler. This woman," Griff began, gesturing to Kyla, "is Kyla Tramontano, Grandmother. Her father is Kyle Tramontano, a Navajo from Chinle. Her mother was Anglo. They divorced many years ago, and Kyla never knew her father. She would like to find him now. Do you know him?"

The old woman's dark eyes narrowed thoughtfully. "Tell me more about this Kyle Tramontano. Sometimes my memory forgets."

Kyla smiled at the woman's choice of words and warmed to her immediately. She laid her hand on Griff's arm, as if to tell him she could handle this. "Kyle was my father, but I never knew him. Although he was from somewhere around Chinle, my mother married him in Albuquerque. He was an artist. After I was born, my mother took me and moved back to Chicago, a city far away to the east. I grew up there and never saw my father. Now that I am an adult, I would like to know him. Can you help me find him?"

The grandmother nodded slowly as Kyla talked. "I knew a man named Tramontano. He lived near the big mesa. He was a weaver. Made beautiful rugs and sometimes did beading for ceremonial dancers. Then he went away to school and learned the white man's way."

Kyla leaned forward and shook her head slowly. "This man was a weaver? Did beadwork? No, I don't think so. My father was an artist."

The old Navajo lady continued. "This man learned to paint pictures on canvas and sell them for much money. Married white woman with yellow hair in Albuquerque. She took her infant and left."

Kyla's eyes grew round with excitement. Could it be possible they were talking about the same man? Surely there weren't many Navajo men who married blond Anglos! "Oh yes! Maybe so! My mother was blond. I could be the baby that was taken away. Was his name Kyle Tramontano?"

"His name was Tramontano." She nodded silently, not offering any more information until probed.

"Do you know where he is now?"

The old woman shook her head and her dark, sad eyes met Kyla's. "He is not with us anymore. He has gone on to the spirit world."

Kyla's shoulders sagged in disappointment, and Griff's arm went instinctively around them. "Are . . . are you sure?"

"He was very sick and came back so the *shaman* could perform his healing ceremonial." She shrugged her withered shoulders. "But he has gone on. I am sorry to have to tell you this."

Kyla sat speechless for sad, silent moments after the old grandmother's final words. It had never occurred to Kyla that her father might be dead. In her mind, he was *somewhere* in the vast Indian country, riding horseback among the barren rocks, watching sheep, painting desert scenes . . . even whittling. But not dead!

Griff spoke, his voice strangely hoarse. "Thank you very much for remembering, Grandmother. It is very important for us to know these things." He stood, towering over the little Navajo lady. Hunching slightly in the low house, he propelled Kyla toward the door.

"Thank you. Thank you." They touched hands with Grandmother Dezbah and Pablo before leaving.

Kyla sat numbly in the Volvo while Griff scrambled in the back seat for a bag of groceries. "I'm going to take her something," he mumbled, half to himself.

She pulled her stricken thoughts back to the present, forcing her mind to function. "Griff, why don't you take a picture of this lady for the book? I'm sure she's one of the few Indians who still lives this way."

"Oh, I know, but, now is hardly the time—"

"Your father would have included her and her home, if he had had the opportunity. I feel sure of it. This is the kind of thing we came for, Griff."

His eyes clouded. "I think we found out what we came for, Kyla."

"Then let's take back something positive. Even if they don't use it in the book, I want to remember this lady. Please, Griff."

He sighed. "Damn, woman! When you set your head on something, you're damned impossible! And sometimes you even make good sense!"

Griff carried a bag of groceries into the house and within minutes was snapping photos of Pablo and his grandmother outside their earth hogan. Afterward, he packed away his camera and climbed into the seat beside Kyla. "Let's go find our campsite, little lady."

She smiled in agreement. "Okay, Cowboy." They waved and drove away in a cloud of pinkish-brown dust.

"You know, of course," Griff explained, "that men used to do the blanket weaving and it isn't unusual for them to still do it, along with beading. It's an art as well as a valuable skill."

Kyla's voice was mystically quiet. "Griff, I can't tell you the strange feeling that came over me when she said my father did beading. It's like . . . it's something in me, too. Innate. Buried. Something I've wanted to do all my life, but just now have found the opportunity through Desert Spirits designs."

"I'm glad we came, Kyla."

"Me, too, Griff."

As the sun set in brilliant multicolored stripes over the vermilion cliffs of Canyon de Chelly, Griff and Kyla chose their campsite. Quietly, they worked together building a campfire, arranging sleeping bags, getting ready for the rapidly approaching night.

Griff paused to appraise their surroundings. "It's very beautiful here." The silence was eerie, yet serene.

Kyla looked around her, a strange look of contentment about her. "I feel as though I belong here, Griff.

As though I've been here before. As though I've always been here . . ."

Griff's arms were suddenly around her, hugging her to his warm chest, long and hard. He held her like they would never part, as if he couldn't bear it. His voice rumbled through her. "I'm sorry about your father, Kyla. I didn't think it would end this way."

"Me, either," Kyla sighed, breathing deeply of Griff's wonderful, masculine aroma. "At least you were with me. And we're together now. I take refuge in that, Griff. Hold me, and never let me go."

Griff held her while the canned chili boiled in the pan over the open fire. He held her quietly, securely, while deep inside he wanted to rant and rave and yell "Don't, Kyla! Don't do this to yourself! Don't depend on me! I'm no good for you!" But he didn't say a thing. He just pressed her to him in silence, basking in her closeness.

CHAPTER NINE

Splinters of pink and gray lights topped the towering cliffs of Canyon de Chelly, casting a magenta glow over the ancient, prehistoric Indian ruins. The rising sun blazed the thousand-foot-high sandstone edifices with shades of brilliant vermilion as it had done for centuries, revealing in its light the remnants of a once-rich civilization. Spirits of "the ancient ones" hovered with eagle-wing whistles and leather-taut drums, shell and feather ornaments, valuable turquoise and beads, the whispered rustle and sway of their garments almost a reality.

Beneath it all, two people slept, wrapped in the warmth of each other's arms, content together. A slight stirring from within the sleeping bag was visible, the beginnings of a ritual as ancient as time itself.

A brown-tinted, feminine hand with slender fingers and rounded fingernails scrolled arched designs over the masculine chest with lazy intent. It tickled the dark auburn hair on his chest and circled each button-hard nipple. The man shifted, drawing the feminine warmth closer to his strength. The brown hand trailed deliberately lower, recklessly searching and taunting.

He sucked in a quick breath as small white teeth encircled his nipples and a serpent's tongue lashed at them. Ah, sweet agony! He lay very still, knowing he was helpless in her power, waiting for more of her witchery. A tightness grew through the center of his being as he realized he would readily relinquish himself as an offering, without a battle, if she would only culminate her incessant torture. Divine sacrifice!

Two soft hands worked now, engrossed in their enticing exploration of his fiercely masculine body. An unavoidable tautening surged into his limbs, unmercifully rendering him weak and defenseless. He was a victim of her mastery. Griff moaned softly at the uncomfortable need radiating from deep inside, urging him awake.

One soft hand caressed his waist while the other followed the dark, hair-lined path past his navel, pausing only to punctuate that slight indenture. Then on to tantalizing his flat belly, driving the need in him to a painful supplication. An unintelligible sound escaped his lips as he felt her warm, moist tongue singe his chest, kissing and bathing provocatively. Kyla paused to dip into his navel, a she-cat intent on her prey.

Her shrewd fingers spread over his sensitive inner thighs, ever moving in circles of blissful anguish. Finally, she slipped a hand under his hips, cupping him tightly. He moaned, a low, animal-like sound, his distress becoming even more acute. She dared to pursue further, grasping, stroking, provoking him to the ultimate. For a moment, he was velvet steel in her strong, persuading hands. Then, with a sudden unavoidable thrust, Griff surged against her, branding that reckless, feminine hand with his burning force. His strength was savage, burgeoning, and he had endured all he could.

"Oh God—" he moaned, barely intelligible.

Kyla met his strength with two firm, willing hands, stroking, encircling, fondling. Both hands were busy, never stopping, always urging, until he feared the volcano building inside him would explode.

"What a way to wake up!" he grated. "A wild she-cat!"

"I want you, Griff. And I go after what I want!" she murmured, darting her tongue devilishly into his ear.

"And you know how to get it, too!"

"Haven't you ever been awakened to loving?" she cooed sweetly.

"Not like this!" A low growl emitted from Griff's chest, and he rolled flat on his back. "Come on! I need you now! I can't wait any longer!"

With the grace of a lithe wildcat, Kyla moved over his body, straddling him with knees beside each thin-muscled hip. He groaned in anticipation, writhing impatiently beneath her. "Come on! Love me, Kyla—" he gasped raggedly, nearly wild with desire.

"I do love you, Griff . . ."

With a vigorous thrust, she seated his burning staff deep inside her. "I love you, Griff, I love you . . ." she sang again and again as she moved rhythmically, slowly, gradually gaining speed and energy. She pumped faster and faster, fiery friction building the fever inside them both until they exploded in a staggering, violent combustion.

Then they were lost in a beautiful world of colored lights and thunder as wild passion erupted in a climax of ecstasy. In that glorious moment, their desires and souls were clasped in love, beyond control or choice or calculated plan.

Griff dozed in total relaxation, still inside her. Slowly he came to, awakened to the glorious world in which they floated incoherently. He had never been awakened so delightfully nor brought to such a fevered pitch. Never had he known such a unity of desires. She wanted him as much as he wanted her. That, in itself, had been stimulating and exciting. She had been a passionate she-cat, not denying her own desires for him. For some reason, it was reassuring.

It was with abashed recall that he knew he had lost control, relinquishing all his strength to this physical release. He recalled her feminine exclamation sometime in the melee of fury. He wondered if he had hurt Kyla in his wild and total abandonment. Was she upset, angry? Had she cried out in pain . . . or joy? She lay very still on him, her arms wrapped around his shoulders, her face resting on his chest, her dark hair spread sensuously over his chest, and he reached up to caress it.

Actually Kyla had met him with near-equal force, passion for passion, wild thrust with wild thrust. She had initiated the act, provoking, tantalizing, driving him crazy. She knew what her provocative behavior did and had admitted that she wanted him. Griff smiled contentedly. It was somehow refreshing for her to be the complete and total aggressor. There was a sense of mutuality between them now, a knowledge that they shared completely in this relationship.

But did they *really* share? Her words . . . *I love you, Griff* . . . came back, hauntingly. *Oh no, Kyla! Don't love me! I'm no good for you!* But, was this love? Love like he had never known? Not protective or domineering or idolizing, but equal, corresponding love? Something wonderful that both of them participated in? That either could initiate?

Or was this just the aftermath of shared passion, satisfying and complete? Was this his reaction to a pleasing relationship with a beautiful woman and the satisfaction of knowing she enjoyed sex with him as much as he did with her?

No, Griff wouldn't give in to love, to anything more than shared passion. After his wife died, he had decided there would be no more love for him. The emotional involvement and the responsibility of a relationship with a woman were too great. He was determined to avoid making that commitment to another woman, even Kyla.

She shifted slightly and pressed a smiling kiss against his chest. "How's that for a morning bracer?"

One of his hands rested on her dark head, the other on her bare hip, sprawled over his loins. He clamped her to him, instinctively trying to maintain what he knew was soon to end. "Oh God! Wonderful! Beats O.J. any day!"

"Hmmm, I agree. We seem to have the same ideas."

"The same passions!" He rolled to the side, cuddling her in his arms. "Vigorous! Did you hear the thunder roll?"

She laughed. "And see the lightning flash?"

He kissed her nose and cheeks and mouth. "Ah, yes, my little she-cat. I knew it wouldn't be a mistake to bring you along! See what good company you are? Not a boring minute!" His kisses dipped to her neck.

"Well, Cowboy, you're in luck this trip. I'll even make coffee for you. How would you like some about now?"

"Coffee?" he chuckled. "Do you mean you have culinary skills as well?"

"I'm multitalented." She smiled smugly and scooted away from his arms. Reaching for a small towel, she cleansed herself, then handed him one. "You wait here, Cowboy, and I'll show you all I've learned about living in the wilds."

"So far, you're at the head of the class! Wildest she-cat I know!"

"I mean about making campfires," she amended.

"Well, you sure kindle my fires," he quipped, then grinned with little-boy devilment. "Sorry, I couldn't resist."

"I think you need a cup of coffee to clear your muddled brain!" she groaned, rolling her eyes at his humorous attempts.

His hand caressed her bare shoulder. "It's muddled with sexy thoughts of you, little she-cat."

She shivered away from his touch, albeit reluctantly, and slithered into a velour robe against the early morning chill. Actually, the garment was more fit for lounging at home than dragging the dusty campground, but it was all she had for warmth. "You stay put and keep my place warm," she advised. "I'll return when the coffee perks. Let's see now. First, stoke the fire." She bent to the dying embers of the small fire.

"I hope you're better at preparing breakfast than you were at supper. It's not easy to burn a can of chili, but you managed to do it last night!" he teased.

She made a face at him, then turned back to her chore. "That, Cowboy, was your fault!"

"My fault?" he retorted, watching her with a growing appreciation. God, she was beautiful in the morning light. A special glow lit her high cheekbones, giving them even more prominence.

"Yep, your fault," she confirmed, watching with elementary satisfaction as the small fire blazed. "You're irresistible, and I'm weak when it comes to tall, redheaded cowboys! I hope you're keeping my spot in that sleeping bag warm. I'll be right back with the water."

Kyla strolled away, her dark hair tumbling past her shoulders, the tail of her dark green robe swaying slightly. She looked so delicate, so vulnerable framed against the backdrop of thousand-foot canyon cliffs. A beautiful image of eons past. Suddenly, Griff was scrambling for his camera, a nude madman turning dials and switching settings. Scampering fingers, clumsy in their haste, snapped photos.

She bent to fill the coffeepot with water, and her tousled hair fell over one shoulder in a rich, sable cascade. The sun-blazed, skyscraping fortress of Canyon de Chelly dwarfed Kyla's tall figure, as it minimized everything in its towering wake. She lifted her face to the sky, as if drinking in the essence of the morning. She belonged there. She was obviously no stranger to this land, even though Griff knew she had never been here in her life. At this moment the spirits of her ancestors were resurrected in her.

Griff was stricken with the realization. Before him was an awsome sight, almost like an apparition. A spirit of the desert. He felt a moment of panic, thinking that if she was an imaginary figure, she might vanish. His practical mind assured him that what they had just shared was very physical, very real. Yet, he felt a desperate urge to preserve this moment, save this emotion that welled inside him. The only way he knew how to do that was with the camera.

Kyla returned slowly, obviously enjoying every moment. Fitting the old-style percolator together, she placed it on the low rack and watched the blaze lick around its bottom. Still on her haunches, she turned toward Griff at the sound of his clicking camera. "What are you doing, Cowboy? Do you know how funny you look?"

He lay sprawled on top of the sleeping bag, nude as a lizard, aiming the camera directly at her. "It's my photographer's blood surfacing. I just couldn't resist. This place—and you—are beautiful. And there is an altogether different perspective from here."

"From flat on the ground? I have a different perspective of you, too!" she laughed. "Maybe there's more of your father in you than you're willing to admit."

He agreed thoughtfully, still snapping photos. "Maybe you're right. I think we're both finding traces of our fathers in ourselves."

"Yes. This trip has revealed a lot about myself," she admitted quietly, then switched from the brief, pensive mood. "Hey! I thought you were keeping my place warm! I want my coffee in a warm bed."

"Me too! And, I am keeping it warm! Just for you!"

She observed the clear knob of glass as the coffee perked, gathering strength and darkness. It was a restful, placid sight, reflecting her mood. "The coffee's almost ready," she announced with pride.

"To hell with coffee! I want you—right here with me!"

"After all this effort, you're getting coffee, whether you like it or not!" She approached slowly, a steaming cup in each hand.

He took the cups and held them, inhaling the aromatic brew while she slipped out of her robe. As Kyla dropped it to the ground, her bare skin was embellished with golden silk gossamer. Her shoulders, her breasts, her thighs shimmered with the sun's highlights. It was a picture Griff would never forget.

"Oh God, woman! You are pure torture for a man to watch! Hurry up and come here to me! And me with both hands full!"

She knelt breathtakingly close, her well-formed breasts achingly close to his occupied hands. "I'll take my coffee now," she whispered, instinctively knowing the bewitching things the sight of her did to him. She loved watching Griff look at her with love in his eyes.

With his free hand he cupped one ecru mound, his thumb stroking the pert bronze nipple. "Kyla . . ."

"I know," she smiled faintly. "Me, too. Hold me, Griff." She took both their cups and placed them beside the sleeping bag before sliding eagerly into his arms. Her pliant breasts pressed ardently against his solid chest, and her bare form molded quite naturally to his. Their hips meshed and long legs entwined.

"This is where you belong, Kyla." One hairy leg crossed over hers possessively.

"This is where *we* belong. Together. Griff, did I thank you for bringing me here? It's . . . it's been more beautiful than I ever imagined."

He gently lifted her breast to his lips. "Beautiful . . ." he repeated. "Kyla, Kyla, I can't stay away from you." His kiss etched her breasts with the passion that was already growing inside him again.

"Love me, Griff. Make me feel wanted. Make me feel like a woman. Your woman." Her delectable breasts grew tight in his hands, glowing in the morning sunlight.

Kyla's words branded him with unquenchable desire, and Griff scooted her firmly onto her back. His arms braced his looming form on either side of her face. "You are my woman, Kyla. And you are definitely wanted!"

He moved astride her, asserting his overwhelming masculine force against her feminine softness. "Oh, yes, Kyla. You are desired . . . you are beautiful . . ." His words were muffled against her ear as he lowered his chest to hers, pressing her breasts to him.

Kyla moaned softly, with the force of his power entering her. "Yes, love me, Griff. Love me . . ."

Try as he might, he couldn't resist her, couldn't prevent this from happening. Once she had him in her spell, he was swept along, completely out of control. He wanted her, only her, now and always. *Always?* Oh God, he would fight that . . . tomorrow. For now, he would have her. There was nothing else to satisfy this burning desire in both of them. In the early morning light, they rose once again to the heights of love's pinnacle.

Later, after a leisurely, unburned breakfast, they spent the day exploring Indian ruins. They hiked through and climbed among the ancient settings of some unknown civilizations. They drove until roads ended, then continued on foot. Griff took innumerable photographs, more than enough to finish his father's book.

Kyla followed his every footstep, feeling surprisingly at ease and comfortable with the new world she was carving for herself. It was now complete. At first it had been disturbing to learn that her unknown father was dead. However, because of their lifelong separation, there was no heavy mourning. And yet, there was a distinct feeling of loss. Of knowing that a part of herself was gone. Of unrealized dreams that would never be fulfilled.

Actually, though, Kyla was grateful to have learned so much about Kyle Tramontano, her Navajo father. He was now very real, not just a dream. She knew more about him now than her mother had ever revealed. Was it possible that her mother didn't know some of these things about him?

Kyla glanced at Griff, climbing the rocks above her, and felt that it was probable that her mother had fallen in love with a man she hardly knew. She and Griff were learning new things about each other with each passing day. Perhaps her mother and father had had a brief liaison, and she had become pregnant. Perhaps . . . oh, how Kyla wished she knew more about their story. It was her story, too! Unfortunately, she would probably never know.

Still, it was comforting to know that her father had been creative, had woven rugs and even designed with beads, as Ed Nah was teaching her now. Kyla realized she was continuing his heritage, her own Navajo heritage, and that was a good feeling.

By the time they left the remoteness of Canyon de Chelly and Chinle, Kyla knew in her heart that she loved Griff. It was a comforting knowledge, yet exciting. He was so different from other men she had known, from Ian. She gazed at his large masculine hands and knew she soared with joy when they touched her. He was rugged, yet caring. Almost gentle. But, strangely enough, it was his rugged cowboy exterior that she responded to so eagerly.

Perhaps it was the same with her own parents. Her mother, suave and sophisticated, had fallen in love with a rough diamond, a rural, hardy man who couldn't—wouldn't—adapt to her city ways. Invariably, she found she couldn't live in his world. So, she had taken her baby and left.

Kyla wondered what would happen if she and Griff faced the same decision. Instinctively, she knew that Griff was like her father in that he would never leave this country. She sighed and rested her head on his shoulder. But they would never have to face that particular decision. She would gladly follow Griff to the ends of the earth. It never occurred to her that he wouldn't want her to follow him.

His hand reached back to caress her smooth cheek with his rough fingers. "What was that big sigh for?"

She closed her soft hand lovingly over his. "Oh, just

what a good trip this has been. And, how happy I am with you. I hate to see it end."

"Then let's prolong it a little. Why don't we spend the night in a motel along the way? We can drive on to Tucson tomorrow. Does a nice hot bath sound good?"

"A nice hot bath and you, Cowboy!" She smiled and kissed his palm, then rubbed it against her cheek.

"With an offer like that, I don't have to be convinced!" He turned in at the next neon vacancy sign.

When Kyla pulled into her driveway late the next afternoon, she was met by Madeline scurrying toward the gray Chevy. Immediately her paranoid mind rebelled. *Oh God, no! Not again! Don't tell me Ian has returned!* She recoiled in the seat, unable to move. As Madeline drew closer, Kyla could see a smile plastered across her face. Surely things couldn't be too bad if Madeline could smile like that. Kyla lifted a hand in greeting and opened the car door.

Madeline beamed excitedly. "Guess what, Kyla! While you were gone, Mavis called. She has arranged another show! This time, we're the featured artists at a convention of boutique retailers at the El Conquistador Resort! This could be IT, Kyla!"

CHAPTER TEN

"What an exciting week this has been! Your stock of Desert Spirits designs is growing again, Kyla. I'm very proud of you." Madeline's blue eyes crinkled with a pleased smile as she watched her friend work.

"Thank you, Madeline. You are my strongest ally. Without your help and support, I could never have made it past this horrendous destruction. Believe me, I had a strong desire to fold it up then. Of course, there's Chansler Marketing and Mavis in particular to credit for keeping us busy with style shows. Sometimes I wonder if we're going to be ready in a month!" Kyla's dark head bent closer over her hands as she concentrated on the intricacy of her task.

"At the day and night rate all of you are working, I have no doubt! How's the beading coming along?" Madeline craned her head to watch the precision beadwork Kyla was producing on a forest-green UltraSuede Indian shirt.

"Ah, the agony before the ecstasy!" Kyla groaned spiritedly. "Ed Nah is a good teacher, but a hard driver! When she declared that we couldn't possibly have an adequate number of garments made in time for the show, I thought it would be a cinch to help her! Now she has us all beading, including the two Indian models! You should see them with their glamorous fingernails, threading those tiny needles and sorting through for irregular beads! They're doing a pretty good job of it, too."

"Looks like you're getting the hang of it," Madeline observed as Kyla's limber needle dug after a tiny, bright, seed bead.

"This is definitely not easy! It takes patience, and lots of it! Not to mention skill. And, it's so damned time-consuming! Yesterday I spent twenty minutes trying to thread this teeny-tiny needle's eye before I could get started! At that rate, I'll never turn a profit! Thank God Ed Nah's faster at this than me!"

"Now you have a greater appreciation of Ed Nah's work," Madeline admonished. "This is good for you, Kyla. You should know all phases of your business, anyway."

"Oh, yes. I have a tremendous appreciation of Ed Nah's work, and I can't wait to turn the whole thing back over to her! I'll take designing and running the business of Desert Spirits any day!" Kyla paused to count the beads lined up on her needle.

"It won't be long before you're running at normal capacity again. It's a shame I can't help with this beading, but my crippled fingers are no good for such intricacies anymore." A brief sadness invaded Madeline's usually sunny face.

"We have other jobs for you, my friend," Kyla assured her pointedly. "And they are equally important. Actually, the upcoming style show and all this overtime work has crowded out my worry over Ian or whoever did that damage."

"Of course, because of him, you're all working overtime to meet your deadlines. Does Griff know about the show? Haven't seen much of him lately," Madeline observed coolly.

"He knows," Kyla clipped and plunged her needle into the fabric with fervor. "Chansler Marketing arranged everything for this upcoming show, remember? Actually, I haven't seen much of Mr. Chansler, either. He's probably just too busy."

"Couldn't be any busier than we are," Madeline pointed out arching her brow.

With an indignant sigh, Kyla rested her hands and gazed out the window. A summer breeze persistently caught the cottonwood branch and made it dance. "I've seen him only once since our trip to Canyon de Chelly. His feelings for me have definitely cooled, Madeline, and I don't know why."

"Ask him. Maybe it's as you said. He's just too busy these days. Open up those communication lines, though, Kyla. You have a right to know what's going on in his head. My problem is, I got so accustomed to having that tall cowboy around, I'm spoiled. He was always available to lift boxes or help in other ways."

Kyla picked up the needle again and began counting beads. "Yes, Griff does tend to spoil you," she agreed sadly. "Did I tell you the insurance man called today? Said I should be receiving a check within two weeks."

"Wonderful! Maybe then you can rent a decent work studio."

Kyla poised the needle and retorted, *"We* can rent one. You're a part of this, too, Madeline. I hope you've done your job and found a place roomy enough for our operations. Since you can't do this meticulous beadwork, I'm placing you in charge of relocation."

Madeline nodded enthusiastically. "I know of an empty building right here in Tubac. It's large and will give our Desert Spirits room to grow. Seems appropriate, too. Already has wrought-iron bars on the windows. They're decorative with elegant Spanish designs, but serve the purpose just the same."

"Bars at the windows?" Kyla frowned and wrinkled her nose. "I don't want to have to resort to bars. That's why I moved away from Chicago! Now, here I am in paradise, and I have to lock myself in! It's an abomination!"

"Why, I thought you came out here to be with me and start anew," Madeline teased softly.

"I did, but I didn't plan on doing it behind bars because of the high crime rate in Tubac!" Kyla explained in exasperation.

Madeline shrugged. "Normally, you wouldn't have to, because Tubac is a very safe, rather sleepy place to live. I think you brought excitement and 'high crime' with you, young lady."

Kyla didn't look up, but she knew what Madeline was thinking. She had considered it, too. A hundred times. Now that they were constructing so many valuable garments, she worried about each piece even more. An unpleasant paranoia was invading her daily life. Quietly, she posed, "Do you really think he did it?"

Madeline pressed her lips together ominously. "I do. Furthermore, I know it's none of my business, but I think you were wrong not to mention Ian to the police."

"But I don't know for sure that he was involved. You can't just throw out accusations with no proof. Ian has no motive . . . besides driving ambition." She laid aside the beaded shirt and began pacing the small tiled kitchen. "I haven't seen Ian in a year. I certainly haven't seen him here in Tubac. All I have is circumstantial evidence that he took our designs. Why in hell would he care what I'm doing? I just can't believe he would bother with me after all this time."

Madeline seethed at her friend's remarks. "Kyla! Maybe you've forgotten what he did to you at Market Designs. After that, I'd believe he's capable of anything! He's highly ambitious and extremely competitive and he knows you have a good thing going in your Indian designs. Perhaps jealousy is his motive. Who knows? I do know one thing though. A credible designer doesn't steal designs. Ian did it once before, then left you to face the investigating committee by yourself and to take the rap. Kyla, he almost ruined your career! Now, he's back to try again!"

Weakly, Kyla admitted to herself that getting away from Ian was the real reason she had come to Arizona. "Actually, he pushed me into starting my own design company. Because of him I did it sooner than I normally would have."

"Yes," Madeline said narrowly. "He put you in the wonderful position of sinking or swimming. What if you couldn't pull this off? Hadn't been strong enough to make it on your own? Where would you be today? Working for Goldwater's planning someone else's style shows!"

Kyla stuffed her hands in her jeans pockets. "But I was lucky. I had you to lean on and provide my financial backing. Together, we're going to pull it off, Madeline. I just keep hoping it wasn't him. I can't believe anyone who cares about designs and beauty and creativity would be that destructive."

Madeline muttered, "Well, believe it! Stop making excuses for him and come out of your gilded cage, Kyla. Ian is an ambitious man, capable of doing almost anything to achieve his goals."

"I guess I don't want to think I fell for such a person," Kyla admitted hollowly.

Madeline nodded forgivingly. "I know. I can understand your feelings. Ian is also a handsome, charming, intelligent man. I'm sure he has a bright future ahead of him. He's just too anxious for success, and he *can* be devious. That's his biggest weakness."

"But still, why couldn't I have seen his weaknesses sooner. Before . . ."

"Before taking him into your confidence?"

"Into my home!" Kyla wheezed bitterly.

"Why? I'll tell you. You were frustrated at work, looking for a way out of the dull routine. Your mother had just died. You were vulnerable, Kyla. He was charming. It could have happened to anyone. Anyway, it lasted only a couple of months."

"Long enough to practically ruin my career. Will he ever leave me alone?" Kyla's voice became a wail, and tears were very close to the surface.

Madeline patted her arm consolingly. "Of course, he will. When you tell the police all this!"

"But"—Kyla turned troubled eyes to her friend—"what if—oh, I don't know what to do. I . . . I think I'll go talk to Griff. He'll know what to do. I miss him so . . ."

Madeline examined Kyla's expressive face, the deep, dark eyes revealing hidden feelings that, until now, she had failed to express. After a minute, Madeline said quietly, "You love Griff, don't you, Kyla?"

Kyla wrenched a tight smile and nodded. "I'm afraid so, Madeline, and I don't know what to do about it."

With a happy smile, Madeline clasped her hands. "Just let nature take its course, sweetheart."

Nature already took its course! Kyla thought miserably. Mustering a wry smile, she allowed, "I've tried to be patient, but he keeps up this elusive dance. When I step forward, he steps backward. He doesn't want me."

"Are you sure you want him, Kyla? He's different from any man you've known. You admitted that yourself."

"Maybe that's why I'm attracted to him. He is different. But, Griff is strong, Madeline. And he has integrity. I admire him . . ." Her voice dwindled and her thoughts took over. *And I can't help loving him. All I know is what happens when he touches me! I fall apart inside!*

"You sound like a star-struck kid!" Madeline scowled. "That's not enough for a lasting relationship. Look what happened to your mother!"

Kyla put aside her beadwork and lifted her chin.

170

"Love isn't enough for a lasting relationship? I'm not like my mother. Not entirely. Remember, I also have the blood and heritage of my father. I think I'll go see Griff . . ."

Madeline placed her gnarled hand gently on Kyla's arm. "Make sure it's what you want."

Kyla's deep brown eyes met Madeline's steadily. "I know what I want! Griff is the one who isn't sure. I just have to convince him!"

An hour later, when Kyla stepped inside Griff's stylish house, she could hear the shower. That's why he didn't answer the doorbell, she deduced. She paused in the living room with outright admiration, unable to bypass his magnificent view of the pool and city nestled between the Tucson and Rincon mountains. It was dusk and lights in the city were beginning to sprinkle to life. Then, on through the adjoining dining room, resplendent with the same glorious view through glass doors. She had eaten at that table with him, after . . . Oh dear God, this house was all so familiar to her. Why did she feel like an intruder? Suddenly, she was a stranger in Griff's life!

Kyla took a deep breath and opened his bedroom door. Oh, God, she should knock! This room held memories, too. Intimate . . . wonderful memories. She started to back away when the shower stopped. She had to let him know she was there.

"Griff?" Her voice squeaked nervously.

Immediately Griff appeared from the large bath and dressing room that adjoined his bedroom. He stood, somewhat surprised, in all his nude glory! Kyla swallowed thickly at the sight of him, tall, handsome, hard muscles glistening with wet beads. Before he could utter a word, his expression spoke loud and clear. *Intruder!* Then, his face changed, softened. "Kyla! What a . . . nice surprise!"

He reached inside the door for a towel and blotted the remainder of moisture from his expansive chest. Then, with a humorous flourish of modesty, he encircled his waist with the thick terry towel, twisting it securely, low on his hip.

For a nervous moment, Kyla was speechless. She knew this man so well. *She loved him!* They had shared so much . . . shared love. And yet, at this moment, she faced a stranger. A nude man who looked at her with a stressful, almost tormented, expression on his face and a towel twisted low on his belly. Suddenly, she felt absolutely foolish. What the hell was she doing here? Was it possible to convince Griff of anything, much less her love?

Why had she just walked into his home? What an arrogant, thoughtless thing to do! At the time, it seemed perfectly natural. Now the only thing "perfectly natural" was Griff's buff-shaded, hairy body.

Come on now, she chided herself. *This is Griff! Your cowboy!*

"Griff . . . I . . ." she began, her voice gaining momentum, her courage gathering spunk. She cleared her throat to start again. "I haven't seen much of you lately."

"I've been busy. The book, you know."

"More trips to Flagstaff?"

He nodded. "A few. How's your work going?"

She shrugged. "Busy, too."

Damn! They were two people who once had been so

intimate and now could barely exchange small talk. What about the caring? The shared joys? The love?

Kyla snapped back to the seminude man facing her. "Would you . . ." she gulped. "Would you get dressed so we can talk, Griff?"

He smiled. "Uh, yes. This isn't the most appropriate attire, is it?"

"It's very disconcerting."

He reached for Jockey briefs in a drawer and slipped them over his slim hips.

"And a shirt, too," she instructed, emotionally racked by the arousing nudity of Griff. Suddenly, the original reason for coming, to discuss Ian's suspected involvement in the burglary, was forgotten. She only wanted to talk about the two of them. He was definitely cooler. *Cold as ice.* She had to know why.

"Griff, I . . . don't know what's happened to us. Things seem to have fallen apart since Chinle. Why?" With a sigh, she slumped to sit on the edge of the bed. *The bed where they had made love.*

Griff jerked a tee shirt over his head. "You're jumping to conclusions, Kyla. Things are still the same between us. I've just been very busy lately. So have you."

With a curt shake of her head, Kyla denied what he was saying. "I . . . I'm having my second show in a month, and we haven't talked about it. Or celebrated. I thought you would care . . ."

"Of course I care," he stated roughly. "I just have my own life and problems right now. I can't drop everything every time you succeed, Kyla. You're going to have a lifetime of successes. And I—"

"You won't be around to help me celebrate? Is that what you're saying, Griff?"

173

"Not every time, no."

His brown eyes couldn't hide the absolute joy he felt for her accomplishments, but his casual demeanor remained staid. No shouts of delight, no grabbing her in a huge bear hug, no sweet, sensuous kisses of congratulations. His jaw was firmly set, and he resolutely stuffed his shirt into dark slacks.

Kyla looked away, fighting tears at his obvious indifference. "Griff, don't do this to me. Don't push me away again. You're turning your back on me. On us. I love you. And I know you—"

"No!" He exploded with more energy than he had felt all week. "Don't—"

"But I do, Griff. I can't help myself. I do love you, and I think you love me. Why are you denying it? We have shared so much. Working together, searching for my father, the beautiful sunsets at Canyon de Chelly, the nights together—" She choked into silence thinking of their lovemaking.

"You're romanticizing things somewhat, aren't you?" he asked. "Don't confuse love with gratitude. I think that's what you're feeling for me now."

"Gratitude?" she sputtered angrily. "I couldn't go to bed with a man just for 'gratitude'! My feelings for you go much deeper than that. Griff, you must know it. Surely you feel what I'm feeling. Why are you denying it?" She reached for his taut arm, wanting, needing to touch him. To cling to him.

As if burned, he jerked away from her touch. "No, Kyla! Don't love me! I'm no good for you! I have too much in my past to be able to let go and love you!"

Wrenching her hands together, Kyla nodded. "I know about your wife. We can deal with that."

"Could you deal with it even if you knew I killed her?" He stared, wild-eyed, at a speechless Kyla for a long moment, then wheeled and left the room.

The silence was deafening as a throbbing in Kyla's ears pounded adrenaline through her limp body. As if in a daze, she followed him.

Griff stood wide-legged, his back to her as he gazed, unseeingly, over his magnificent view of the city.

She tried to steady her voice. "Griff? What are you talking about? Your wife died in an auto accident." There was a desperation to her tone. Surely that was the truth. Surely he hadn't actually killed her! What kind of man had she fallen in love with?

"I was driving," he muttered in dull tone. "I was responsible for her safety. Her death was my fault. She didn't die in the accident. She lived for three months. Three painful, heartbreaking months when she couldn't move, couldn't speak, couldn't function on her own. Only her eyes watched me, accusingly. Everything else was paralyzed. Those tormenting eyes . . ."

"Oh Griff . . . I'm sorry." Kyla licked her dry lips. "How terrible for you."

Slowly he turned toward her, his face full of pain. "Shari finally died, three months after the accident. Pneumonia, they said. And you know something horrible? I was relieved! Can you believe it? I was damned relieved to know my own wife had died. To escape those eyes!"

"Yes, Griff, I can believe it. I think your reaction was a normal one. It must have been a relief to know that someone you loved was finally out of pain."

"But I didn't love her anymore." The words echoed

hollowly. "Our marriage was over. We just played a game, waiting for a reason to end it. Instead, I made her life hell until she died. I killed her, and she knew it. Her eyes told me."

"And you bought that whole guilt trip." Kyla could hardly believe her sharply accusing words. But she couldn't sit quietly and let the man she loved take this unreasonable blame.

"Don't talk to me like that!"

"Why not? Hasn't anyone told you that you're carrying around a burden of guilt that you don't deserve?"

His brown eyes lashed harshly at Kyla. "What about Shari? She didn't deserve her fate! Oh, I've been over this a million times in my mind! Don't think there haven't been many sleepless nights! The facts are, I'm alive and she's dead because of something I did! That's hard to forget!"

"No, she didn't deserve her fate," Kyla answered quietly. "But you shouldn't be blaming yourself. Her death wasn't your fault. It was a regrettable accident. And you can't change it. It's over now, Griff. Put it away. Start anew. Let yourself love. Love me, Griff . . ."

He shook his head. "I can't. I can't commit myself to another wife. You deserve better than what I can give you. Don't you see? I would be no good for you."

"Right now, you're no good for anyone, including yourself," she flared with something close to anger. Or was it extreme desperation? She knew, deep in her heart, she was losing him.

"You're right," he admitted softly. "So you

shouldn't get mixed up with someone like me, Kyla. You have too much going for you."

"I'm already mixed up with you, Griff. I already love you, regardless of your past." She faced him squarely, sure of her words, positive of her feelings.

"Well, I feel sorry for you, Kyla. You're wasting your time on me." Griff's brown eyes caressed her, briefly, then he gained control and turned away. Brushing past her, he bolted out the door, leaving her alone in his stylish, foothills house.

Kyla sat stunned.

She could hear the Jag start up, hear Griff roar away in the night. The Tucson city lights blinked peacefully, outlining the mountains with their reflections. Kyla stared for a long time, barely seeing, her mind numb.

Then the tears came. She had lost him, maybe driven him away with her damned aggressiveness. Why did she have to approach him tonight? Maybe if she had waited, hadn't been so eager to go after him . . .

Kyla cried, great heaving sobs shaking her shoulders until she felt empty. Lonely, alone, and empty. Devoid of tears and feeling.

Finally, in the dark of night, she left and drove home. Home to Tubac and her new business and her solitary life. She knew now that she would have to proceed without Griff.

It was an empty, gut-wrenching feeling.

She pulled into her Tubac driveway beside a strange car. Kyla's broken heart was in her throat as she shoved open the kitchen door.

CHAPTER ELEVEN

Kyla flung open the door with ill-gotten courage. She *knew* who was here! Knew even before she saw him! And she wouldn't let him destroy her again! The kitchen drawers were thrown open, and various utensils were strewn across the counter and table. Obviously, he'd searched her old hiding places for new sketches.

"Ian, what are you doing here?" She walked into the front workroom and peered incautiously at the slender man whose dark head was bent, intent on his search. Every desk drawer and cabinet door in sight was open, their contents scattered!

A swell of inflammatory anger surged inside Kyla, and it was all she could do to keep from railing viciously at him. How dare he invade her privacy? And make such a mess. Why, everything was a wreck.

Then a sickening fear struck her. *Had he seen the new creations?* Kyla's dark eyes cut alarmingly to the locked closet which contained the newest garments, then back to Ian. With relief she noted that the doors were battered, but remained locked. Why was he doing this?

"Ian?"

This time he looked up, somewhat surprised, yet not uneasy that he had been caught in the act. A wild thought crossed Kyla's mind. Perhaps he wanted to be caught . . . by her!

"Kyla, darling! How wonderful to see you again!"

"Don't 'Kyla darling' me when you've just broken into my home!" she fumed. "Just what do you think you're doing?"

"Well, I'm not stealing anything!" He smiled pleasantly. He was so damned calm! And, of course, still handsome. "I'm checking to see what you're up to, my darling. You're awfully busy for such a small operation. Any why are you stuck way out here, so far from civilization and a broad market for distribution?"

"What business is it of yours what I'm doing, and where I'm doing it? Ian, this"—she waved her hand toward the riotous room—"is unforgivable! Why are you trying to ruin me?"

He stood and stuffed his hands, with long fingers, into his pockets. Ambling around the desk, he continued to smile, his lips curling above the dark lines of his beard. For the first time, she could see him as he really was. He took on a sinister appearance to Kyla and suddenly she hated him. "I'm not trying to ruin you, Kyla darling. I want you to succeed, but . . . with me."

"With you? What are you talking about?"

"I want to make you a little proposition. Come to

California and work with me. We can combine your little business with mine and distribute from there."

Her back bristled at his "little business" comment, but that was the least of her worries. "What gall! You break in here and steal my originals, then have the moxie to make such a preposterous offer? Work together? Forget it!"

He stood very close and folded his arms across his chest. "We were once dynamite together, Kyla. We could be again."

The only dynamite Kyla knew was that building inside her, and she feared it would go off any minute. Somehow, she instinctively knew she should remain calm with Ian. Calm and collected. She shook her head. "I'm sorry, Ian. It's over between us. I could never work with you, especially not after what you did to me in Chicago, and now stealing my newest creations. I could never trust you."

"This little episode?" He smirked. "Your originals are safe, packed away in California, just waiting for you. Anyway, that was nothing, compared to what could happen."

"Are you threatening me?" She managed to control the shaking in her voice, but her entire body quaked with rage as he actually admitted his guilt.

"I'm just trying to persuade you to come around to my side. You'll never be successful here." He gestured to the adobe-walled studio.

"You'll see to it," she blanched, turning from his hard glare. Hugging her shaking hands to her ribs, Kyla took a couple of steps toward the kitchen. Her instinct for self-preservation urged her to get away from him.

She noticed the stainless-steel knife on the kitchen table, and her heart lurched with a new fear.

Ian's voice commanded, "Open those closet doors, Kyla. Unlock them."

Wildly, she wheeled around to face him, knowing instantly she couldn't leave him here! He would force the closet open and take her designs again! She couldn't possibly let that happen! Wouldn't! Gone was her earlier composure as her voice rose hysterically. "No! I won't give you another chance at my creations! They're mine! How dare you think you can come in here and steal my work and make demands of me?"

In a flash of a movement, he grabbed her arm. "I said, open it! I want to see what you're hiding!"

"We have simply replaced what you took. That's all," she grated between her teeth.

"You're lying! I know you have more, and I want to see them!" His grip on her arm tightened, and his long fingers dug fiercely into her skin.

"See them?" she mocked, realizing she was inflaming him with her taunting, but was unable to stop herself. "You're not laying a hand on my clothes again. Your raging ambition has changed you, Ian. I can't believe I ever cared for the likes of you. I never want to see you again! Get out! You're despicable . . ."

With her final words, Ian's open hand whacked her across the face with such force that she staggered backward. Oh God, she had pushed him too far! Her face stung fiercely, as he lunged angrily to hit her again. Kyla had never dealt with physical violence before and, for a moment, she was stunned by the act.

She realized vaguely that if she didn't do something

Ian would hit her again. But her mind was working in slow motion, and her body failed to respond.

He struck again, this time leaving the side of her face numb. Frantically, Kyla backed away, trying to escape. Ian's threatening eyes were steel flint, cutting into her with a frightening glare. What was this man capable of? She could actually be fighting for her life, and a voice inside her screamed *protect yourself!*

In a brief flash of panic, Kyla prayed for Griff to burst into the room, to save her from Ian's viciousness. That's what happened in the movies. The hero returned just in the nick of time. But this wasn't the movies and Griff was no longer a part of her life. This was real, and there was no one to save her from Ian but herself.

As she scrambled away from him, Kyla's buttocks rammed hard against the table which blocked her escape. *Protect yourself!* Instinctively, her free hand reached behind, her fingers closing around the handle of the knife. *The knife!* It would be her protection! *Or her own destruction!*

Suddenly, there was a tangling of arms and legs, a scuffling of feet! There followed the inevitable struggle, then a woman's scream and a man's curse! Then blood, splattering, dripping. An agonizing groan. Then silence.

The kitchen door burst open. "Kyla? Kyla, what's going on? Are you all right? Oh, my God!"

Kyla's voice rose weakly from where she lay on the floor. "I saved them, Madeline. I saved the new designs. But, oh God, I think I killed Ian!"

Both women turned stunned, frightened eyes to the slumped male figure lying facedown near Kyla. Blood spilled sickeningly from Ian's body to the tiled kitchen floor.

"I know this sounds crazy, Madeline. And Griff would laugh and say I was romanticizing too much. But I kept wishing Griff would walk through the door. I fantasized him bursting dramatically into the room and saving me!" Kyla chuckled as she and Madeline shared coffee the next morning.

"And, instead, you got me." Madeline smiled. "Sorry I wasn't Griff, my dear. But when I heard those screams and saw that strange car, I didn't think I had time to call Griff or anyone!"

"You didn't. I was so glad to see you, Madeline!"

"I know you must have been scared, Kyla. I never dreamed Ian could be so vicious."

"I have never been so scared in my life," Kyla admitted. "I still can't believe I picked up that knife. Thank God the blade missed his spleen." She raised the icebag to her left eye, which was colored an ugly reddish-purple.

"Yes," nodded Madeline. "And he'll live to face charges on everything from breaking and entering to assault and battery."

Quietly, Kyla confessed, "I'm glad you didn't call Griff."

"Why? Is he out of town? He'll certainly want to know about this."

Kyla shook her head firmly. "No, he won't care."

"Won't care? What are you talking about? Of course he will! Look at you, Kyla! You could have been . . ." She gulped heavily, unable to finish. "You could have

183

been hurt badly. I can't believe you haven't called him yet."

"Madeline, Griff and I . . . we're through. It's over between us." Saying it aloud sent a mournful wave through Kyla.

"I . . . can't believe it!"

"And don't advise me to tell him how I feel. I did that. Last night, before coming home to Ian and this chaos here, I told Griff I loved him. And he told me he didn't, couldn't, love me. That's it." She stood and poured herself another cup of coffee with a slightly shaky hand. Saying it aloud made it seem so real. So final. But that's what she needed. To believe it. To make it real. To go on with her life without hoping for the impossible.

"Well, I don't believe him!" Madeline protested. "I think he does love you. He's just not willing to admit it yet."

Kyla smiled at her friend. "You're romanticizing the situation, Madeline. I appreciate it, but it doesn't help me face the truth—that he wants nothing else to do with me!"

"I warned you, Kyla. He's . . . he's just too different from you. And you fell for that rough cowboy exterior!" Madeline sputtered. "I wish I could talk to that big stubborn cowboy! I'd set him straight!"

Kyla's hand shot out to grip Madeline's wrist. "Oh no! Please don't do that, Madeline! Don't—"

"Not to worry, Kyla," Madeline assured her. "I won't interfere. I wouldn't dare. I probably have said too much already. But I hate to see you hurt."

"Thanks, Madeline. But it's over. He walked away. He turned his back on me, and, obviously, I don't need him anymore . . ." Kyla's voice trailed weakly as she remembered their last conversation. *You're wasting your time on me!*

Kyla filled the next lonely weeks with work. She repeatedly scrubbed the bloodstained tile floor until there wasn't a trace of Ian's blood left. She beaded with Ed Nah, planned with Madeline, even sewed with Carmen. Occasionally, she imagined seeing Griff outside her door. It was always a mirage. A trick of her mind.

The nights were the loneliest time without Griff as she lay in bed and imagined herself safe and warm in his strong arms. It seemed like eons without him.

He didn't burst through the door when he returned. Instead he knocked politely, then called her name.

Kyla laid aside the intricately beaded shirt with a jolt as she recognized his voice. Griff! Demanding every nerve in her body to calm down, Kyla opened the door. There he stood, tall, imposing, damned handsome. Her cowboy. Only, he wasn't hers anymore.

"Kyla," he began in a rush of questions, "are you all right? Was Ian here? Is this the man you told me about? Did you really stab him?"

She nodded, gripping the door-facing with nervous white-knuckled fingers. "But it wasn't exactly a stabbing, more an accident."

"I've been out of town, and it scared the hell out of me when I read about it in the papers. What happened?" Instinctively his fingers softly traced the bruised violet-colored skin around her eye. His hand then dropped down to her forearm just above the yellowish traces of an ugly bruise. His thumb unconsciously circled in small, loving caresses.

His sensuous strokes touched Kyla all the way to the center of her being, and she felt weak with desire for this man who loomed in her doorway. This man who didn't love her. She wanted to scream, *Don't touch me unless you mean it!* But she didn't want the touching to end. Yet, end it must, and she had to be the one who broke it up. She couldn't stand it, otherwise.

"Would you like to come in?" Maybe if they sat in separate chairs he wouldn't be tempted to touch her in false consolation. He doesn't really care, she reminded herself.

"I thought you'd never ask." He stepped inside, and she noticed a large manila envelope in his hand.

"Have a seat. I'll fix us some iced tea."

"No . . . thank you. Kyla, let's talk. I have something to say. But, first, I want to hear about Ian. Everything that happened. You look terrible."

She smiled faintly. "You should see the other guy."

"Worse, I hope."

"Much," she nodded and sat at the table, folding her hands to hide her nervousness. "Well, Griff, you said you couldn't escape your past. I guess I couldn't, either. Ian thought he could force me to go into business with him. If I lost my business, I'd turn to him. He intended to make sure my business failed. That was his motivation from the beginning."

"Are you sure he wasn't a jealous lover?" Griff spit the words out.

Kyla shook her head honestly. "I don't think so. His motives were purely monetary. You see, he had some brilliant ideas. And he admired my work when we were in Chicago together. He thought that if I failed badly enough here, I would have to turn somewhere for work. And he planned to be there with an offer. We could combine our forces and become dynamite together, as he put it."

"And the knife?" Griff pressed.

"That was actually my fault."

"You? You aren't that aggressive! Nor are you violent!"

"No," she admitted. "But I learned that I could defend myself if I had to. It was a frightening realization to know that I was capable of violence, if the situation was right. Ian scared me badly. Threatened me. He . . . he hit me a couple of times and pushed me against the table."

"The S.O.B.—" Griff raged, unable to listen quietly.

"The knife was lying on the table," Kyla continued, somehow feeling a release with the retelling. "I . . . I went blank. The only thing I could think was 'protect yourself.' "

Griff's hand slid to cover both of hers in a gesture of concern. She wished he would keep his hands to himself.

"Oh, God, Kyla, I could kill him for hurting you—"

Kyla searched his hard, brown eyes with a puzzled glance. "I almost did, Griff. We struggled, and God only knows how Ian got stabbed. I certainly didn't overpower him. It just . . . happened. He's recuperating under guard at Tucson Medical Center."

"And you?" His hand slid to encircle one wrist.

She shrugged. "I'm still a little paranoid, but I'll make it."

"Yes, I know you will. You're a strong gal. But I

should have been here with you. I hope we can salvage what we had together, Kyla."

Her eyes shot up to question his. "W-what?"

"I've done a lot of thinking these past couple of weeks. I've examined my feelings for you, truthfully for a change. And you were right. I've been fighting them."

Kyla raised her chin guardedly. She had her own feelings to protect here. She couldn't look at their relationship lightly anymore. "What made you realize that?"

"First, the news about Ian. I saw red when I realized you'd been hurt. Then, there's this." He drew something from the flat yellow envelope. "I've spent the last few days in Flagstaff with Northrup Press, finalizing the details on my father's book. They astounded me by wanting to use one of my photos for the cover."

She smiled, genuinely pleased. "That's wonderful, Griff. I knew all along, you were good. You have more of your father's talent than you care to admit."

"You'll be pleased to know my editor has included the photo you insisted I take of the old Navajo woman, Dezbah, and her grandson, Pablo, beside their hogan. But this photo they chose for the cover . . ." He shook his head. "It's of you, Kyla. They said it depicted both the contemporary Indian, in your image, and the ancient traditions, with the stark Canyon de Chelly in the background." He shoved the photo in front of her, then continued. "I took one look at it and knew I couldn't agree to their request without consulting you."

She peered at the black and white print. Actually,

upon viewing it, one would never know the identity of the person whose image was caught. Nor could one tell if she actually was an Indian. Only she and Griff knew the truth.

The woman's back was to the camera, her head turned to the side, her long, dark hair falling over one shoulder. She was squatting down placing a container near the campfire, and even the container was indistinguishable as a regular coffeepot. Her figure was dwarfed by towering walls of sandstone, overwhelming and ancient. In a compositional sense, the photograph was powerful. And symbolic. It projected a spirit of beauty that reflected the past and present at the same time.

Trying to be objective, Kyla could see why Northrup chose it. However, the sensitive memories the photo evoked almost overwhelmed her, and she struggled with her torn emotions.

One look and she remembered their morning of lovemaking, sweet and sensual. Complete and fulfilling. Never to be forgotten. She recalled their jokes and laughter. She could see Griff's humorous posture as he lay naked snapping photographs. There was the abandoned coffee and more lovemaking. A huge wedge of sorrow rose within her, for all that was lost now. It was all she could do to remain straight-faced.

"Why does it matter what I think? It's your photo, Griff. You can do with it whatever you want. You don't need my permission," she announced coldly. It was the only way she could deal with the situation. Her hand snaked out and pushed the photo back toward him.

"But, it . . . it means too much to me." Griff's

voice was strangely quiet and strained. "It was taken the morning we made love, Kyla. I just couldn't let the intimacy that it represented to me go public without consulting you first. And I must know if it means as much to you as it does to me."

Tears of unchecked emotion glistened in her dark eyes. "Of course it does, Griff. It's just . . . well, you're romanticizing this too much, aren't you?"

"Even cowboys can be romantic. Sometimes it just takes us a little longer, that's all."

"Griff, what are you saying?"

"That I was wrong. I do care for you, Kyla. Very much."

"Oh, Cowboy, I love you!" In a spontaneous motion, Kyla rushed to his arms, kissing his lips with unabashed vigor.

When he could catch his breath, Griff claimed, "You're the damnedest, most aggressive female I've ever known! You didn't even give me a chance to say I love you first!"

She sat in his lap and wrapped her arms around his neck. "What's wrong, Cowboy? Haven't you ever had a woman make the first move?" Her hands moved up his chest seductively.

He grinned, his voice rough and low. "Once. In a remote canyon. She was a wild seductress who looked a lot like the woman in this picture. Like you, Kyla. My love . . ." His arms slipped around her back and clasped her securely to him.

"Madeline said we were too different. But I knew you'd come back to me. I just had to wait. It was the hardest thing I've ever done. Waiting is not my style." She smiled sweetly.

"Nor mine. I want you now, Kyla. I can't live without you any longer . . ." His kiss encompassed and delighted her as he stood and swung her up into his arms.

Later, snuggled against his wonderful bare body, she murmured, "I've never been so happy, Griff."

"Do we have time for a honeymoon on some remote Mexican beach before your big show? I know a beautiful little place where we can be all alone . . ."

Kyla laughed, feeling giddy with happiness. "If we can slip away before Ed Nah shoves another shirt for beading into my hands!"

"I have other things in mind for your hands, my little she-cat. I want you in my arms and my life forever, Kyla."

"Oh Griff . . . yes!"

He murmured loving words against her dark hair. "I'm willing to put my past behind me with your help. I love you . . ." He buried kisses against her temple.

Kyla nodded and rested her head contentedly on his shoulder. "We both have pasts to forget, Griff. We'll forget them together. My lovable cowboy . . ."

"And we have a beautiful future ahead. My precious she-cat . . ."

Now you can reserve January's Candlelights _before_ they're published!

- ♥ You'll have copies set aside for *you* the instant they come off press.
- ♥ You'll save yourself precious shopping time by arranging for *home delivery*.
- ♥ You'll feel proud and efficient about organizing a system that *guarantees* delivery.
- ♥ You'll avoid the disappointment of not finding *every* title you want and need.

ECSTASY SUPREMES $2.50 each

- ☐ 57 **HIDDEN MANEUVERS**, Eleanor Woods 13595-8-13
- ☐ 58 **LOVE HAS MANY VOICES**, Linda Randall Wisdom 15008-6-50
- ☐ 59 **ALL THE RIGHT MOVES**, JoAnna Brandon 10130-1-37
- ☐ 60 **FINDERS KEEPERS**, Candice Adams 12509-X-28

ECSTASY ROMANCES $1.95 each

- ☐ 298 **MY KIND OF LOVE**, Barbara Andrews 16202-5-29
- ☐ 299 **SHENANDOAH SUMMER**, Samantha Hughes 18045-7-18
- ☐ 300 **STAND STILL THE MOMENT**, Margaret Dobson 18197-6-22
- ☐ 301 **NOT TOO PERFECT**, Candice Adams 16451-6-19
- ☐ 302 **LAUGHTER'S WAY**, Paula Hamilton 14712-3-19
- ☐ 303 **TOMORROW'S PROMISE**, Emily Elliott 18737-0-45
- ☐ 304 **PULLING THE STRINGS**, Alison Tyler 17180-6-23
- ☐ 305 **FIRE AND ICE**, Anna Hudson 12690-8-27

At your local bookstore or use this handy coupon for ordering:

Dell DELL READERS SERVICE – Dept. B465A
P.O. BOX 1000, PINE BROOK, N.J. 07058

Please send me the above title(s). I am enclosing $_____ (please add 75¢ per copy to cover postage and handling). Send check or money order – no cash or CODs. Please allow 3-4 weeks for shipment.
<u>CANADIAN ORDERS:</u> please submit in U.S. dollars.

Ms./Mrs./Mr _____

Address _____

City/State _____ Zip _____